A CHANGE
IN
THE WIND

Books by Leslie Waller

THE FAMILY

THE BANKER

PHOENIX ISLAND

A CHANGE IN THE WIND

A CHANGE
IN
THE WIND

BY

LESLIE WALLER

Bernard Geis Associates

NEW YORK

A CHANGE
IN
THE WIND

By 1927 a widespread neurosis began to be evident . . . contemporaries of mine had begun to disappear into the dark maw of violence. A classmate killed his wife and himself on Long Island, another tumbled "accidentally" from a skyscraper in Philadelphia, another purposely from a skyscraper in New York. One was killed in a speakeasy in Chicago; another was beaten to death in a speakeasy in New York and crawled home to the Princeton Club to die; still another had his skull crushed by a maniac's axe . . . these were my friends; moreover, these things happened not during the depression but during the boom.

In the spring of '27, something bright and alien flashed across the sky. A young Minnesotan who seemed to have had nothing to do with his generation did a heroic thing, and for a moment people set down their glasses in country clubs and speakeasies and thought of their old best dreams. Maybe there was a way out by flying, maybe our restless blood could find frontiers in the illimitable air. But by that time we were all pretty well committed; and the Jazz Age continued; we would all have one more.

F. Scott Fitzgerald
(Echoes of the Jazz Age,
Scribner's, 1931)

Chapter 1

All day the wind had been veering slowly from the east to the northeast. Now it was sweeping in off Great South Bay in long trumpeting blasts that flattened the marsh grass along the water's edge. The wind cried softly as it combed up over the ridges of the sand dunes facing the Atlantic, then hit hard into the downdropping curl of the surf, scattering cold spray along the strand.

On this part of Fire Island only the seabirds really knew their way, the gulls and terns, and perhaps the small, wiry red foxes and starved jack rabbits. Harry Regan had cut all the trails through this tangle of bayberry, poison ivy, and holly bush. The rare visitors—Coast Guard search parties mostly—knew the lateral trail along the ocean behind the swell of the dunes and the bay trail through the bleaching driftwood and clamshells. But the crooked trails Harry had cut from shore to shore the few blocks from the Atlantic to the bay were known only to him and to the gulls veering high overhead on this cold May night.

The seven-tube superhet radio crackled with sharp bursts of static. Harry sat beside it in the small living room of the shack, his fingers slowly tuning the variable condenser as he tried to tease words into the headset clamped over his ears.

"I'm just a kid again," a baritone sang bouncily, "doing what I did again, singing a song. When the red, red robin comes—"

Harry twisted the big black knob with its vernier markings. The living room of the shack was vibrant with heat from the potbelly stove. Inside it, driftwood chunks burned fiercely. Across the room Maeve sewed and rocked.

". . . face, you've got the cutest little baby face . . ."

Harry Regan grimaced and continued to tune the radio. At five minutes to eight, Horgan sometimes tried a signal on the regular broadcast band.

"Two sandwiches," a voice in the earphones said with abrupt clarity, "two canteens, and two chocolate bars. But Slim Lindbergh apparently has his mind on other matters as he wings his lonely way acro—"

Harry twisted the knob through another short arc. His attention was diverted for a moment by the ripples of motion in the battery jar fluid behind the radio. Then he realized that Maeve's motion in the rocking chair had caused the ripples.

". . . but you forgot to remember."

He tuned out the thin, tinny, meaching sound of the tenor's voice and immediately got another news broadcast. ". . . the world continues to wait with bated breath while the intrepid young barnstormer and mail pilot makes a valiant attempt where so many have failed to—"

Harry glanced at his wristwatch. No signal on the broadcast band. Perhaps Horgan was late, by an hour or a day. That was the trouble with their system of signals. "Gimme a little kiss," a woman begged, "will ya, huh? And I'll give it right back to y—"

Harry winced and kept tuning. "What is it, love?" Maeve asked.

Her voice shook him. She was too young to have such a voice, such a low, thrumming voice with such power to stir him. He pulled off the earphones and grinned at her. "This mad Lindbergh."

"Why do you call him mad?" Maeve's dark hazel eyes were shielded by thick lashes as she continued to look down at her sewing.

"Because he'll kill himself the way the other six did." Harry glanced at his waterproof wristwatch. "Almost eight o'clock. I'll try now."

He put on the earphones again. Under the table on which the huge radio lay were some extra coils, enameled copper wire strung on open cores of wood. Harry attached the leads from one coil to the Fahnestock clips in the rear of the radio. He adjusted two more sets of wires, attaching them to new binding posts. Then he hooked on an additional pair of battery jars. Slowly now, frowning,

5

he began to tune the radio through a new frequency spread, well beyond the broadcast bands, to a new setting.

His watch showed exactly eight o'clock. At that instant, the headset earphone came to life with something other than static. Distinctly, Harry heard the dot-dash-dot-dot.

He watched his wristwatch as he tuned carefully to another setting. After a minute had elapsed, he heard the old Morse letter X once more, dot-dash-dot-dot. Now he tuned to a third frequency and, in a minute, heard X again.

Quickly, Harry switched the radio to its hornlike loudspeaker, disconnected the short-wave attachments, and got to his feet. "It's tonight," he said.

Maeve's eyes looked immense as she stared up at him. "You'll be out rounding up the boys now."

"Won't take but an hour or two."

"More like till midnight, Harry."

"And if it does?"

"That's what I mean." Maeve's head went down. Harry watched the way the fine long black hair glistened outwards from a radial point at the top of her head. "And I won't see you till sunup."

Harry took a short, sharp breath of annoyance. "That's so."

"If I see you alive at all," she added in a voice so soft that the moan of the wind almost drowned it out.

Harry got down on his knees in front of her, took the sewing from her hand, and threw it to one side. "Oh, you'll see me alive," he said. He grinned up into her face

6

and, reaching out, rubbed the fine red hairs on the back of his hand up and down across her cheekbone.

She smiled slowly and moved his hand from her face to her breast. She began to unbutton her cardigan sweater as Harry's hand caressed her. The light blue denim man's shirt underneath the sweater pulled open and her small breasts burst into the orange-amber light from the kerosene lamp on the wall.

Harry's mouth closed hard on one nipple and his hands began to stroke down her waist, sliding her skirt off. He plunged his tongue deep into her navel and sent a tremor across the muscles of her belly. Then he bit hard into the mound of shiny black hair and her scream of joy made the skin across his shoulders bristle. He could feel her thighs tighten almost painfully around him as they rolled to the floor, gasping and laughing.

The loudspeaker sizzled. Voices came and went. ". . . two flashlights, four red flares, five cans of rations, and a hacksaw blade. Meanwhile, at Roosevelt Airfield, officials gave the Lone Eagle less than a two-to-one chance of . . ."

Her sharp howl of climax reached him from far away, over great distances of warmth and movement as he felt the tumid thrust of his penis kindle suddenly. "Christ, Harry!" she whispered. Her breath hurtled in and out of her like the bellows of a furnace. "Harry, I'm . . . Harry, I'm coming again."

". . . liners and freighters along the North Atlantic shipping lanes have been advised that rescue . . ."

This time they climaxed together and Harry felt the hard knot burst inside him and the tide roar out with the headlong rush of an express train, harsh and thunderous.

". . . either a May twenty-first that will go down in the splendid annals of aviation or the dismal pages of defeat as the first . . ."

"Will you for God's sake shut your gob?" Harry asked the loudspeaker. He lunged across the room to switch off the radio.

"Harry, you have no soul," Maeve said. "To pull out smoking hot, all hard and wet." She crawled across the room toward him like a cat. He started to disconnect the radio's batteries.

"One alone," the loudspeaker moaned, "to be my—"

Harry twisted savagely at the dial. "Let it play," Maeve begged. "Let it play a bit longer, sweetness."

He tuned to an instrumental number, all creamy saxophones playing tight, mewing chords while the brass section did something rhythmic with plunger mutes.

"As if it mattered a hoot in hell to the human race, such as it is, if Lindbergh makes it or not," Harry muttered. He sank down in the chair, legs sprawled. "They don't deserve him. The man has solid guts, but they don't deserve to be shown what a pond their miserable ocean is. Mind you, I think it's grand, him doing it, because it has to be done. But, God, they don't deserve to have it done for them, they don't. Christ, Maeve, will you leave off? I'm not nineteen any more. Will you save it, Maeve?"

She looked up at him through the thick fringe of her eyelashes. "Save it for what?"

He took advantage of the interruption to pull away from her, stand up, and move off toward the door as he fastened the metal buttons of his dungarees and buckled his thick leather belt.

"If I listened to you, Maeve," he said, yanking a thick black turtleneck sweater over his head, "I'd've left the Island long ago to be a street car conductor in Brooklyn or something grand like that and you'd not only hate me but you'd be bored out of your lovely head as well."

"But at least I'd be Mrs. Harry Regan."

He turned up the edge of the black knit watch cap and pulled it down on the crown of his head. "A place for everything," he said, "and everything in its place."

She started for him on her hands and knees. Harry snatched up the old Parabellum 9 mm. automatic and its holster hanging over the window and kicked open the door.

He stood in the doorway for an instant. The music from the radio's loudspeaker segued blandly into a different key and a different tempo. A tenor began to throb guiltily.

"What can I say dear, after I say I'm sorry? What can I—"

Harry's laugh drowned out the tenor. He grinned lewdly at Maeve and dashed off into the cold wind of night.

He had less than four hours now to round up boat crews and have the craft waiting offshore in fifty fathoms of Atlantic by the time midnight struck.

Chapter 2

On a mid-May night, the village of Ocean Beach seemed deserted. The immense whale of a ferryboat made the trip from the mainland of Long Island once a day in summer and half a dozen times on weekends during the season. But not in May. May was still not the season.

Like the lone cottages along the far sweep of dune and the ones that hugged the shell-strewn bay beach, like the isolated driftwood shacks at the far eastern end of Fire Island, the village of Ocean Beach gave the appearance of being almost unpopulated. It would until the middle of June. Until then, only year-around natives, or a few city dwellers with island homes that had to be readied for the season, would be found in Ocean Beach.

And out-of-work actors. Only one light showed along the narrow sidewalk that led from the ferry mooring on the bay through tangles of blueberry and holly to the crest of the dune overlooking the Atlantic. At this late hour, the cottages were dark except for the big white house with the second-story walk-around porch. It had been set just back of the dune grass with its face turned toward the crashing ocean.

A faint light showed in its living room windows. At sea, ships might barely distinguish the three squares of light the house showed them. More likely, the candlelight from the hurricane lamps was too dim.

Inside, Goldie Fain found another hurricane lamp, pulled up the glass chimney, and lighted the candle. It did little to improve the dark-paneled look of the room. She scratched her head, digging her long nails into the scalp at the back where her hair was thickest.

At that moment she heard a horse's hoofbeats along the hardpacked damp sand near the water's edge. She strode to the window and stared out into the night, squinting.

"It's not him, Goldie." The thin man with the aquiline nose and narrow face watched her for a moment. He waited patiently for her to turn back to him.

He had known her for nearly ten years now. They had never played together, of course. Goldie's first commitment was always to Ziegfeld. She would drop any project to appear in the newest Follies and seemed to spend the time between vegetating off-season in her Ocean Beach house.

It was not impossible, of course, that Paul Lachaise might do a musical comedy, a revue, even one of Ziegfeld's extravaganzas. But he didn't quite see himself doing it since it wasn't very clear what else a Shakespearean actor did except Shakespeare. O'Neill, of course, but the damned stuff was infinitely harder to act than Shakespeare.

With the Bard, as Lachaise had long ago found out, one didn't actually have to make the words into complete sense. One turned loose the criminally gorgeous instrument of one's voice, mouthing the luscious syllables and stressing the meter in an offbeat fashion, and both the audiences and the critics felt they were in the presence of a major talent.

"I said it's not Harry Regan," Lachaise repeated.

"S'not what?" Goldie turned back and posed for a moment exactly between two hurricane lamps, getting the full up-from-under lighting that gave her rather ordinary face, with its too-big mouth, an intriguing Oriental cast.

Lachaise grinned maliciously. "Step a little closer to the lamp on the right, darling," he suggested. "It minimizes that lit-tle crook in the bridge of your nose."

He upended the bottle and watched the last half ounce of Scotch splash into his glass. "Nifty, kiddo," he murmured. "The last of the coffin varnish."

"No more," Goldie said. She had given her usual stage pronunciation a rest in favor of her native New York accent, which made "more" into "mow-uh."

Lachaise was glad, in a way, that she didn't feel called on to be anything but natural with him. They had been sleeping together, off and on, during the past ten years in periods when they weren't sleeping with other people, or their various respective spouses. Lachaise felt that if he had a single friend in the world, it just might be this stupid, ignorant, lovable bitch.

"You're completely enameled as it is," she went on. "Just because I lay for a bootlegger, it doesn't mean I can keep pouring sheep dip down that throat of yours forever."

"But surely there is another bottle somewhere in this mildewed mansion?"

"Another bottle?" She gave Lachaise a sample of her idiot laugh, the one she used in Dumb Dora sketches. "The cellar is filled with cases. This Regan bozo is using me as a depot."

"He's no dumbbell."

Goldie stared at Lachaise for a moment, squinting slightly as she had when staring out the window at what might have been Harry Regan on horseback. Lachaise knew her to be horribly nearsighted and too impossibly vain to own even a secret pair of glasses.

"Don't screw up those melting Jewish eyes that way."

Goldie made a face. Twenty rows back in the orchestra, in the mezzanine, even in the far reaches of the balconies, audiences without opera glasses could clearly distinguish every feature of Goldie Fain's famous faces. She had a repertoire, Lachaise knew, of at least a dozen. The one she was making now looked new to him, a kind of cross between a petulant owl around the eyes and a disapproving camel around the nose and mouth.

"You look utterly disgusted."

"With you, you shiftless bastard."

Goldie strode back to the wicker sofa, her long white crepe de chine lounging pajamas with the bell bottoms flouncing wildly. She flopped down on the sofa cushion and continued to glare at Lachaise.

"I should have known better," she said, "than to hole up this week with a lounge-lizard actor. All you ever talk about is booze."

Lachaise sketched a light, witty gesture of the kind he had introduced into his 1925 *Hamlet*, the one that sold out so regularly on matinees that the management had put in a third one.

"Booze and boozing," Goldie went on.

"Instead of what?" Lachaise asked. He watched her brain almost visibly at work, conjuring up an answer. She would be tremendous in movies, he felt. Nothing was ever under wraps with her. She had no internal life. Everything showed.

"Instead of serious things," Goldie said. "My God, Paul. I mean, my God, this is a crazy world we're living in. Look at Lindbergh."

"No crazier than we are."

"What about Bob? Wasn't that the craziest thing?"

Lachaise frowned. Something had happened with Bob Benchley the previous week or so, but he hadn't paid much attention.

"Do you believe him?" she persisted. "I do."

It came back suddenly. Benchley and some others had filed affidavits in Massachusetts, swearing Judge Thayer had secretly promised to hang Sacco and Vanzetti. "I believe him," Lachaise said then.

"It's crazy. Americans don't do things like that. The judge should step down."

Lachaise shook his head. "Should but won't. Times are changing, kiddo. The country's changing. Look at Nicaragua."

"But for a judge to—" Goldie gestured helplessly.

"The whole trial and appeal has run down," Lachaise said. "They'll fry. It's been seven years, everyone's fed up, and they'll fry."

"You make it sound like a play with a bad last act. Quick curtain."

"That's it." Lachaise got up and began prowling the room, opening cabinet doors and poking behind bookshelves. "Where? Where?"

"You see?" Goldie demanded. "You can't continue a decent conversation for more than ten words before you're off on the gargle again."

Lachaise whirled on her, his hawk profile glinting in the candlelight, his head held at precisely the correct angle to emphasize his more menacing qualities. He thought he might have a go at Sherlock Holmes or perhaps Jekyll and Hyde. It would be a change from the Bard. "Why the hell would any red-blooded cake-eater want to talk to a flapper like you, baby," he asked, "when we could be humping ourselves to death between those sea-damp sheets of yours?"

It might even be worth doing Fu Manchu. You could get a lot of mileage out of a juicy villain. Of course, with a nose like his, he'd have one hell of a time as the Yellow Peril Incarnate, but . . .

"Wh-why are you looking at me that way?"

Lachaise lifted his hands, fingers drawn back like talons, and bared his teeth very slightly. Dracula was another possibility. Always a dearth of really talented vampires.

"Paul. Cut it out."

He made his eyes widen. He knew from years of watching himself in mirrors that he now had a complete ring of white around each iris. He smiled softly at Goldie and reached for her throat.

" 'Speak of me as I am; nothing extenuate,
  Nor set down aught in malice: then must you speak
  Of one that loved not wisely but too well.' "

Goldie pulled back from him. His fingers groped for her neck. "Listen," she said. "Listen, Paul. I mean, you—"

" 'I kiss'd thee ere I killed thee; no way but this,
  Killing myself, to die upon a kiss.' "

"Paul!"

He pulled her up out of the sofa by her neck and planted an immense kiss on her mouth. Then he thrust her from him and plunged an imaginary dagger into his heart. "Augh!" he coughed. "Augh!"

"Sweet Christ, will you leave me alone? There's another bottle in the desk. Top right drawer."

" 'For this relief much thanks; 'tis bitter cold,
  And I am sick at heart.' "

"Paul, is it possible for an actor ever to give one good hot damn about anything but his own miserable skin?"

Lachaise opened the drawer and busied himself peeling the lead foil from the cork of the Johnnie Walker Black Label bottle. "Your Harry Regan does you well, Goldie."

"I do him okay, too."

"I'll bet you do. Some of the tricks you taught me." He laughed.

"What about the ones you taught me?" Goldie started to giggle. "You remember where you hid the maraschino cherry that night at the Traymore?"

"Took me half an hour to retrieve it." Lachaise bit down on the cork and plucked it out. He let an inch of whisky pour slowly into his glass. " 'Soup of the evening,' " he sang, " 'beautiful soup.' "

"But Harry's different from you," she mused. "He doesn't get tired of it in the good old-fashioned ways."

Lachaise sipped the warm Scotch and shrugged. "That I can always do with my wife."

"How is she?"

"Not bad." He paused. "Oh, you mean in general? Well." He stared into the glass. "You wouldn't have any ice?" Goldie shook her head. "The wife's fine enough. But . . ." His voice died away.

"But you can't remember which one she is," Goldie finished for him. "I love you, Paul. You're the husband every girl ought to have. Good-looking, sexy, and absent-minded."

"Am I still married to that what'shername opera singer?"

"You know goddamned well you are. The coloratura."

Lachaise nodded. "Thought so." He finished the Scotch in his glass and replenished it. "And you're, uh . . ."

"Between. Betwixt and between." Goldie fluffed out the thick hair at the back of her head and began scratching at it again. "If a girl has Harry Regan and you, what does she need being married?"

Lachaise sat down heavily on the far end of the wicker sofa. The whisky was beginning to do its job. He could feel his lip stiffen slightly. He nodded and sipped from his glass again.

"For a girl who only wants serious talk, you pick the wrong kind of playmates," he said then. He could hear the slurred pronunciation. "Sirrus talk." He frowned. Then he smiled.

"Harry's got a lot more on his mind than you'd imagine," Goldie said loyally. "A hell of a lot more to worry about than his own skin."

"Let's give Harry Regan a rest," Lachaise suggested.

"Let's you give his booze a rest."

"Dumb Jew slut."

"Thanks, rumdum."

"Banana oil."

"Bastard."

"So's your old m . . ." Lachaise began to snore. A moment later the sound awakened him, but he kept his eyes closed. A change in the feel of the sofa cushion under him told him Goldie had gotten to her feet.

He let his eyes open very slightly. Yes, he'd been right. She was standing at the window again, holding up a hur-

ricane lamp in a classic Delsarte pose. He listened, with
her, for hoofbeats, heard none.

She had always had a weakness for crooks of one kind
or another. He supposed Harry Regan to be a rather
superior one in his own way. Maybe there was something
in it at that. Jimmy Valentine. Raffles. My God, one
couldn't go on playing Shakespeare forever.

He watched Goldie press against the glass, as if willing
Regan to ride past. He supposed it was a form of mad-
ness.

"Canst thou not minister to a mind diseas'd,
  Pluck from the memory a rooted sorrow,
  Raze out the written troubles of the brain?"

Lachaise smiled very slightly as he ran over the lines
again in his mind. Then he stood up from the sofa and
bellowed:

" 'And with some sweet oblivious antidote
  Cleanse the stuff'd bosom of that perilous stuff
  Which weighs upon the heart?' "

Goldie gasped and whirled on him, clutching her left
breast. "Do you have to scare me out of my wits?"

Lachaise lifted his glass. " 'Sweet oblivious antidote.' "

"Go to hell."

He nodded solemnly.

" 'Therein the patient
  Must minister to himself.' "

They both heard the hoofbeats then. The sound rattled
briskly and died in the roar of surf as quickly as it had
come. Lachaise wondered if he'd dreamed it.

Chapter 3

Lt. Ashley's shirt had been laundered and starched so many times that the khaki color had faded to a beautiful silvery beige. The heavy fabric was only a shade darker than the twin bars pinned to one point of his collar and the Coast Guard emblem pinned to the other point.

He sat now near a third-floor window of the station, alternately watching the angry surf in the faint half-light of dusk and the two specialist's mates working the control panel of the giant receiver. Overhead the chill May wind tore at the guy wires of the transmitter mast. Ashley stood up.

The movement relieved some of the tightness of the stiff khaki collar around his neck. The reddish skin that had surged out over the top of the starched collar relaxed now and grew pale. It was not that Ashley was plump. It was simply that to him the uniform looked

neater and more Coast Guard when the collar was a half
size too tight.

He paced rapidly behind the two men working the controls. His highly polished black shoes with their leather
heels drummed an impatient tattoo on the wooden floor.
Ashley did not miss seeing the look of annoyance that
passed between the two Coastguardsmen. He knew he
was bothering them. Ashley conceived of his duty as
being, in some part, the harrassment of his men to stimu-
late the greater performance of their own duty.

"Anything?" he snapped.

"Nothing but Lindbergh stuff, sir. It looks like he just
might—"

"Keep combing that kilocycle range."

"Yes, sir."

"Keep shifting to the shorter-wave range, too."

"Yes, sir."

"And don't lose any time shifting back and forth."

"No, sir."

Ashley knew he had already given the two men these
instructions. He also knew, in a general way, that even
without specific instructions the men would perform
pretty much the same on their own. Certainly Heydt
would. But if the world were to be ordered in that on-
your-own fashion, Ashley told himself, there would be no
need for a structure of grade and rank, no need for officers and enlisted men or for distinctions between them,
no need, in fact, for a world organized pretty much along
the same lines. And, while it was certainly true that

Spanier and Heydt, the two men, probably knew as much or more about their jobs as he did, organization was one thing and anarchy another. Their simple, limited excellence at what they did gave them no overview of the total job to be done. This, Ashley knew, was his responsibility and, if he did acknowledge it himself, it was a particular specialty for which he had achieved considerable recognition.

He walked to the window overlooking the ocean. Less than a mile from the Coast Guard station, the tall, black-and-white striped thrust of the Fire Island Lighthouse was barely visible in the gathering dark. As Ashley watched, the light swung quickly past, raking his eyes with a yellow intense enough to make him wince.

He turned from the window only to find himself staring into the hot yellow curlicue of the nearest unshaded clear-glass electric bulb. He shut his eyes. The two images burned for a long moment in his retinas.

He opened his eyes and stared in the direction of the surf. At this hour he could see almost nothing of it. But its shuddering roar, muffled by the thick walls of the station, came to him repeatedly, steadily, with a rhythm he could remember from his earliest years on this misbegotten barrier beach.

Ashley supposed, as he stared into the thickening night outside the window, that it was his familiarity with Fire Island that had first brought him to the attention of his superiors. This forty-mile stretch of beach, deserted except for the summer months, had become a wide-open door for thousands of cases of contraband a month each year since the Volstead Act had been signed. Only in the past year, since Ashley had been assigned the beach command, had any real success been achieved in swinging that door even partly shut.

Ashley began pacing behind the Coastguardsmen again, rapping out an impatient drum roll with his heels.

"Anything?"

"No, sir."

"Don't tell me that. You've heard something, damn it."

"Yes, sir. Just more Lindbergh news. The air's full of it."

"What about code signals?"

"No, sir. Just weather advisories from Barnegat Bay Station."

"Not Coast Guard business, I mean any other signals."

"No, sir."

"Keep at it, then."

"Yes, sir."

"And look lively."

"Yes, sir."

Ashley turned on his heel, pleased at the look of badly concealed hatred on Spanier's face. Good, he told himself; let them know they served a bastard. He had decided the day he'd arrived here that since he wasn't too much older than most of the enlisted men, only a good healthy hatred would keep them in line.

Ashley walked across the radio room to the back window and stared at the very faint smudge of light along the western horizon. According to his own private calculations the code signal for the third week in the fifth month was G. The only signal his men had picked up, and this had been a single transmission at a minute after eight tonight, was the International Morse letter L, a dot, a dash and two dots. L meant absolutely nothing as a delivery signal. It probably signified some change in plans. In any event, when the scouting cutter returned tonight at ten o'clock, it would give Ashley a report on any suspicious shipping outside the three- and twelve-mile limits.

He thought he could detect an unusual number of whitecaps across the surface of Great South Bay even by the faint light fading now along the horizon. The bay itself could easily defeat even the powerfully engined ships of the rum fleet. Shallow and weed-clogged, the bay could be roiled to fury by any wind over 25 knots. And if Ashley was any judge of the howling guy wires overhead, the wind had hit at least 30 knots already. As the nearest thing to a native, he prided himself on reading the wind better than any anenometer. Ashleys had been reading the Fire Island winds for a century and a half.

The first Ashley in these parts, he recalled, had arrived in a double-ended dory from Connecticut about 1790. It had been a traditional clinker-built craft hand-hewn from New England yellow pine. Those first Ashleys on Long Island had been boat builders. As they drifted cross-Island toward the Atlantic shore, however, they turned to clamming and oystering in the bay and to seineing for

bluefish and bass along the outer reaches of the conti-
nental shelf where the coastal waters deepen sharply to
oceanic dimension.

Ashley's grandfather had been a successful farmer, the
last of the breed that harvested the rich, salty marsh grass
once prized as winter fodder for the horses that pulled
wagons and city street cars. Ashley's father, however, had
been counted an alcoholic in an era, just before the turn
of the century, when the average working man consumed
several quarts of beer a day and not a few two-ounce
shots of corn whiskey.

As he stared out at the bay now, Ashley felt the pain
in his lower gut flare suddenly like a Very signal, hot and
red, shooting skyward in the night of his insides. He
grimaced, careful to hide his face from the Coastguardsmen behind him at the control panel. Ashley knew it was
exactly the wrong time for the pain to flare up. Per-
versely, the knowledge seemed to inflame his gut even
more.

He had been afraid to go to a Coast Guard medic,
afraid he might be discharged as unfit. The private doctor
he had gone to, secretly, on his return to the New York
area a year ago, had given him an unfamiliar name for
the pain. Ashley had expected to hear about ulcers. But
the name had been colitis. The doctor had seemed very
serious about it. "Mr. Kramer," he had told Ashley, calling him by the name Ashley had given, "in Japan people
die of colitis. The diet doesn't protect their intestines. Our
diet gives us a little more protection, but not much."

The doctor had not been too helpful. He knew next to

nothing about the disease. This ignorance he cloaked in pomposities like "Medical science hasn't isolated the cause of colitis, Mr. Kramer, but . . ."

Ashley's jaw gritted tight shut now against the grinding hot pain as he turned slowly from the window and walked with some dignity out of the third-floor radio room. He made his way slowly down the stairway to the officers' quarters and shut the door of his room behind him. Still moving with very deliberate slowness, he loosened his black tie, unbuttoned his collar, and opened the bottom drawer of the plain pine bureau.

The alligator-leather travel case he had bought in Panama City two years before lay under a neat line-up of washed and starched shirts. Ashley unlocked the catch and took out the hammered silver flask he had bought in Santo Domingo last year. At the sight of it, the pain in his lower intestine shot forward like a kick. He fell back on the cot and nursed his abdomen with both hands.

Then he unscrewed the cap of the flask and poured three quick swallows of Dewar's down his throat. He groped in the alligator-leather case for his aspirin bottle, shook out three tablets, and swallowed them with another belt of whisky.

The alcohol etched its way down his throat. He gagged for a moment. Sweat broke out in great drops across his forehead and temples. His flaxen hair, neatly brushed sideways from the middle, grew dank with moisture. Hands shaking, Ashley closed the flask and locked it away in the case with the—to him—equally telltale bottle of aspirin. An officer didn't show pain any more than a Coast Guard officer on anti-smuggling duty detail drank captured contraband booze.

After a while, after a long while, the agony began to ease slightly. Instead of a sharp, stabbing pain, it was subsiding to a dull ache that made Ashley feel as if someone had spent time stomping on his abdomen with precision and care. He wondered why the pain always seemed to kick up when he thought about his father. It was almost as if the memory of the drunken old shit would trigger off a pain that required Ashley to take the only whisky he ever drank. It was as if the germs or whatever they were in his colon lay in wait, dormant, ready to ambush him when the recollection of that miserable, sodden prick crossed his mind.

Ashley lay back on the bed and nursed his abdomen again, rubbing it slowly with the fingers and palms of his hands. He knew that some day the pain would grow too great for the aspirin and booze to handle. He knew it would become unbearable and he would do something foolish and desperate. They would find his silver flask and then they would find the place down the beach back of a dune, a foot under the sand, where he had buried the rest of the case he had stolen from the last successful capture. They could recheck the manifests and reports. They would find a one-case discrepancy. They would put two and two together and Ashley would be court-martialed, dishonorably discharged, ruined.

Ashley stared at the single, clear-glass electric bulb

overhead, hanging by a fabric-sheathed wire from a ceiling outlet. The filament's brightness burned into his retina and he let it. He wondered about this and decided the faint pain in his eyes would help mask the receding ache in his gut. Damn the doctor and damn his colitis, Ashley thought. What kind of man told you a name and not a cure?

The only good thing about what was happening tonight, Ashley decided, was that it had taken only one aspirin-and-booze treatment to quell the pain. A month ago, when he had visited his mother in Patchogue and listened again to her endless complaints about his father, the pain had been so bad that it had taken three separate treatments—nine aspirin in all and most of the flask of whisky—to get it under control.

He wondered now if there would ever be a time when his mother would give up the dirge of complaint and let the stink of his father's memory slide quietly under. The old days were gone. The times were changing. The man was long dead, a drunken hero of the Meuse-Argonne.

All that long October, only nine years ago, Ashley and his mother had watched the papers for news of the breakthrough. Pershing's regiments had driven straight into the heart of the German forces and forced a general retreat that ended in armistice. But Ashley's father had stopped two Mauser bullets—chest and throat—on November 10 as he led a charge against a machine-gun emplacement. It had not been heroic enough for the Congressional Medal of Honor, but the Distinguished Service Cross still hung in Ashley's mother's home in Patchogue. Ashley had always believed his father to have made the charge in a moment of booze-sodden frenzy.

He could hear footsteps coming down the stairs and along the corridor to his room. Ashley tried to force his body to move quickly, to realign itself in a posture more fitting for an officer. One of his men couldn't be allowed to find the C.O. sprawled on his bed like a common drunk.

"Excuse me, Lieutenant," Heydt's voice broke into the room's silence. Ashley stood up, swaying sideways for a moment with the sudden shift in posture.

"What is it, Chief?"

He watched Heydt's absolutely smooth face, the rather wide jaw set firm and unmoving, the eyes perfectly motionless as they drilled into his, the mouth quite still. Unlike Spanier, Ashley told himself, Heydt was adept at hiding his hatreds. It was just as well. As Chief Petty Officer, Heydt was the ranking enlisted man in the station. Only Ensign Jorgensen stood in line between Heydt and Ashley in the chain of command.

"Well?" Ashley prodded him. The man was taking too long. Was that a slight flare to Heydt's nostrils? Was he smelling Ashley's breath?

"Beg pardon, sir. We've picked up no new signals, sir. Just that Lindbergh's been aloft more than seventeen hours now. That puts him almost halfway across."

"What's that to me?"

"I thought you might want to—"

"The hell you did, Chief. You just wanted an excuse to snoop around here and find—"

Both men stood silently, listening. Through the rhythmic pounding of the surf, over the moan of the wind, they could hear the hollow thudding of a horse's hooves along the packed wet sand of the beach.

"Christ!" Ashley muttered.

"He's out tonight after all," Heydt said. "And he doesn't mind letting us know it, either, the little red-headed bastard."

"Maybe he's just visiting somewhere."

"Not pushing that horse so fast," Heydt said.

"It may not even be Harry Regan's horse."

"Who else at this time of night?"

They eyed each other for a moment. Ashley moistened his lips. "Other people own horses along the beach."

Heydt's expressionless face looked, if anything, even more deadpan.

"Yes, sir. Will that be all, sir?"

"No. Get a two-man detail out in the beach buggy. See if they can pick up any tracks. See if they can trace Regan's route. Or whoever it was we just heard."

"Yes, sir."

Ashley turned away from the Chief. The pain started in his gut again. "You'd think by now my requisition for horses would have come through. Headquarters has had it six weeks. They know we can't overtake Regan in that beach buggy."

"Not without breaking an axle or two in the pot-holes."

Heydt's face showed a very faint smile, Ashley thought, around the outer corners of his eyes. "I don't suppose there's another Coast Guard unit on this whole Atlantic shore that's put in a requisition for cavalry geldings."

"Too bad," Ashley snapped. "Maybe that's what they need up at the Cape and down along Hatteras. The rum boys run rings around us, sea and land."

Heydt's eyebrows elevated a fraction of a millimeter. "Yes, sir. Will that be all, sir?"

"For now." Ashley waited till Heydt's footsteps had died away. Then he sat down on the edge of the bed, cradling his abdomen in his crossed forearms like a pregnant woman easing the strain on her belly.

Bad. The pain was back and it had grown worse. This was going to be as bad as the visit to Patchogue last month. Ashley unscrewed the flask and gulped at the Scotch. In the distance he could hear the whir-whir of someone cranking the magneto on the beach-to-shore telephone.

He wondered who would be calling whom at this hour. After a while, he took two aspirins and washed them down with more whisky. The flask was almost empty. It was going to be a bad night.

Chapter 4

Maeve had put away the dress she was sewing. A chipped enamel kettle of water squatted on the wood-burning stove in the little shack. The iron, glowing blackish-red under the kettle, made the water inside hum softly and fizzily, like a baby after feeding. But it would be a while, Maeve knew, before it came to a boil.

She stood at the small three-paned window that faced toward the ocean. Because the shack lay low to the sand and well down the back slope of the dune, she could not see the water, but only an imitation of it in the faint, waving line of coarse dunegrass, shuddering in the pale light of the moon.

A low-lying, filmy cloud half covered the moon as it rose in the sky, sometimes blotting it out, sometimes letting the moon concentrate all its bluish force on the poor, shivering blades of grass.

Maeve hugged her forearms. She intended to make herself a great pot of tea so strong it would eat out the insides of any but an Irishwoman. She intended to stay up until that bastard Harry got home, even if the sun were to be coming up when he did so.

Her mother, who had warned her against Harry Regan, had warned her that tea too strong could bring on all kinds of misfortunes, miscarriages, biliousness, early menses, even freckles. When Maeve left home to live with Harry, she had consigned this kind of wisdom to the same ashcan in which she had dumped the rest of her family's advice.

This act of self-liberation, a year ago at nineteen, would not have been possible in a well-brought-up girl, Maeve felt. Her own upbringing left a lot to be desired, especially after Harry had discussed it with her.

"You're being trained as a body servant for the old hag, is all," he had explained. "You're to suffer the fate of so many darlin', juicy Irish lasses. You're destined to wither like a dry stick in the God-fearing service of your sweet Ma throughout her eternally declining years."

After a year of Harry's too-clear vision, commenting on life and people, Maeve supposed she knew him better than most people did, better than anyone else, for that matter, even the other women he slept with. To them he gave temporary pleasure. Her he lived with and cherished as his own. Maybe.

Harry had seen through them all, mother, father, five hoodlum brothers, all of Maeve's family. "They're smugglers, right enough," he patiently explained once, "sons and grandsons of smugglers, to be sure. But never have I seen a more joyless, oafish, Baptist brood of Irish smugglers in me entire life, Maeve, darlin'. Where's the sheer exuberance? It's a business to them, like shoe-clerking. As a label on a photo of the likes of them, the holy word smuggler is disgraced utterly."

Harry had his own ideas of what the Irish should be. Born in the States, he had higher notions about joy and generosity and honor than anyone from across the sea. Yet he was Irish. To the death.

Maeve shivered. She pulled the curtains and turned from the window. Without watching the kettle, she listened to its purr. Bad luck to think of death tonight.

She could picture Harry's laughter at her superstitious ways. He wasn't particularly big, like her father or brothers, but his laugh was huge enough. She imagined Harry stood about five-ten or so and he'd have to be called thin, no doubt of it.

He had the broad sharp chin, the high freckled forehead and the long upper lip of the Irish. His eyes were a strange green-gray-blue. His red hair was a short, coppery scribble across his head and his voice could be anything he wanted of it. He could sing high and talk low, with or without the brogue. He could even talk like a Britisher.

Maeve knew his work in England was best forgotten. It was one of the bad parts of Harry's past life. For a man of thirty-five, he'd had his share of bad years, but the ones to come were going to be better.

She had tried telling him once, not more than a few weeks before, that his fate on earth was to find her. Just that, nothing more. And her fate was to give him joy. Only that.

Harry had scoffed at the whole idea. Remembering, Maeve sat down in the rocker and stared at her small hands. She held joy for him, if he would only take it. But Harry didn't really believe he was fated to be happy. In so many ways he was a spoiled priest. If it wasn't that he hated God—or didn't believe in him—Harry would have made a good priest and her own life's fate would never have been completed.

Wasn't it part of the calling that a man believed in his fellow men? Sinners they were, but he had to believe in their salvation, surely, or there could be no call.

Like most Catholic girls, Maeve had thought of becoming a nun. It was a vain thought, she knew, because she loved the pleasures of her body too well to bury them. But when she'd been younger, she'd toyed with the idea. And she knew how important it was to the sisters who had taught her and her classmates, hellions and imps that they were, to believe that the girls could yet, some day, achieve a kind of perfection.

She suspected Harry had once had that same vision. His bitterness had to spring from somewhere; maybe it had come from the death of that vision. It had started, most likely, with his grandfather.

The old man had come over in one of the famine years, 1845 or thereabouts. The ship's hold had room among the casks for thirty or forty people. But the owner had packed three hundred Irish into the hold, with their meager bit of food, and locked the hatches on them. For a month, they died in their own puke and shit, the old ones and the babies, until two hundred of them had been dumped in the ocean like garbage. Young and strong when he started the voyage, the grandfather had stepped onto the shore of the New World a walking skeleton in search of a crypt.

Instead he found work as a mason's helper in Brooklyn, grew a potbelly, and spent his last years filling young Harry with the treachery, the insane cruelty, the greed, and the deceit of the English. Harry learned the whole story: Cromwell slaughtering Irish peasants by the tens of thousands, the Battle of the Boyne, Wolfe Tone's uprising, and every unsuccessful struggle from Emmet's revolt to the Fenian rebellions of the 1850's.

What kept it so bitter-green in his mind, Maeve knew, was that Ireland still wasn't free, even as the old man filled the boy with the history of his people.

The kettle started to boil. Maeve poured water in the teapot, sloshed it around, and poured it out. Then she spooned tea into the pot and poured the rest of the boiling water over it. After her first cup, she knew, the tea would be black as homemade sin, but she didn't care.

She stood waiting for the tea to brew and thinking of the boy Harry had been, head filled with the sorrows of Old Erin. She recalled that he'd been to college, but whether or not he'd earned a degree she didn't know. She only knew that some ten years ago, when he was twenty-five, Harry had shipped across as an able seaman and jumped ship in Dublin.

"Ah, God, Maeve, the town was in ferment like a keg of ripe berries." That much of his time in Ireland he was willing to remember. The martyrs of the 1916 Easter Rebellion had been buried a year or so and the land was bubbling with plots. At first Harry had found it hard to be accepted by the native Irish, but soon he had gotten involved in the election of 1918, when the Sinn Fein under De Valera won so many seats that they walked out of the British parliament and set up one of their own.

"It was a grand, pure idea, the Dáil Éireann," Harry had said, "a rare thing in this world, the truth made flesh. It had fools and knaves in it, but in the eight hundred years since Henry II stole the Green Isle from us, it was the first time the Irish could govern the Irish. Sinn Fein, 'we ourselves.'"

He'd been unwilling to go on. But Maeve remembered enough of her father's talk with his cronies to know that the Dáil had been powerless as long as the British still controlled the police. "Wasn't there a man named Collins?"

"Mick Collins." The admission came slowly, like a confession.

"It was him declared war?"

Harry had shaken his head. "Not war. In the Philippines they have a Spanish word for it. Guerrilla, a small war. A guerrilla war was Michael Collins's way; striking in the night and fading by day into the landscape."

37

That was as far as he would want to recall. He would mutter about the fat merchants crying shame and the ass-licking bishops threatening excommunication, but he would go no further with the tale. "Ten times I nearly left Ireland," he would say. "Ten times I would have gone home to Brooklyn. Ten times I stayed because we might put it over. And, in two years, I aged ten."

"From the Black and Tans, was it?" Maeve would prod.

Harry would shrug unhappily. Over the months, as Maeve pieced things together—and there wasn't all that much to piece because he spoke of it so sparingly—she came to realize that the Tans had been in Ireland only a year or so. And Harry had been there still, after they left.

No, it hadn't been the Tans. It was something peculiarly Irish that Harry shied away from remembering too clearly, something Irish that finally poisoned his sweet priest's vision of human perfection.

Maeve poured steaming mahogany tea into a white china mug without a handle. She sat in the rocker and cradled the mug, letting the warmth seep into her thin fingers.

Something Irish it was that drove Harry from Ireland and set him wandering the earth, sailing the secret line between crime and the law. Maeve sipped her tea, trying to summon it up for herself. In the absence of Harry, the puzzle of him would have to suffice.

Chapter 5

The place had always gone by the name of the Dutchman's. It was the only German restaurant in all of Islip, or in the greater part of Long Island's South Shore for that matter, and so of course the name was more or less inevitable.

In this case, however, the big three-storied dark red stucco building with its brown half-timbering had actually been built during the war by a Hollander named Boersma. It had not been a particularly good moment in history to open a German restaurant in the United States, and, even though Boersma was of Allied nationality, the potato and hay farmers along the shore refused to make the distinction.

After the advent of Prohibition, a man named Heinckel bought the place from the bank that had foreclosed Boersma's mortgage. Heinckel's connections were good. His beer was strong. His whisky was genuine and so was his gin. To his customers he was just another kind of Dutchman. Nearly everybody came to the Dutchman's, including most of the sheriff's deputies. It was the place to see and be seen and you didn't have to worry about the booze.

When the telephone rang at the far end of the long mahogany bar, Heinckel himself answered. "I'll see if he's here," he murmured into the phone and set it down as he surveyed the room. Although Heinckel was in his fifties, his face was relatively unlined, padded from within by hard, suety fat that kept his cheeks bulging and sallow while it ringed his eyes with ridges of pale white flesh. Most of his customers, he saw, were down at the other end, listening to news of Lindbergh on the radio.

His little eyes settled finally on a small, thin man standing alone halfway along the bar. The man pushed away from the bar to walk toward the telephone. He moved like an ex-jockey, quickly but carefully. When he picked it up, he held the mouthpiece against his lips to muffle his voice.

"Yeh?" He listened for a while. "Probably midnight." He listened again. "You sure about the signal?" He had the accent of the city, not the shore, and he made "sure" into two syllables: "shew-uh." He nodded at the phone. "Worth a try." The first word came out "waith." He replaced the earpiece in its forked cradle and went back quietly to his place at the bar where he drank his beer and waited to catch Heinckel's eye.

The owner moved ponderously along the stretch of

polished mahogany, swabbing it with a wet cloth as he made his way toward the small, thin man. "Another beer, Maxie?"

"Neh." Maxie eyed him. "Pass it aroun', okay? Eleven o'clock out at the Moriches place."

Heinckel's tiny eyes darted sideways, checking on eavesdroppers. The radio crackled and squawked. "One crew or two?" Heinckel asked.

"Many's you can send." The small man lifted the almost empty stein to his lips and finished the last of the beer. He licked a mustache of foam from his thin upper lip. "Four trucks, Whites. None of them lousy Macks. I want speed."

Heinckel stared at the Black Forest cuckoo clock on the wall behind the small man. "Lot of trouble for me to go to just for one phone call, Maxie."

"The info's straight."

"It's almost ten o'clock now. How you expect my boys to get to Moriches in an hour?"

Maxie smiled. "It's easy. Stop dogging it and start roundin' 'em up."

"You sure the tipoff's good?"

"Horse's mouth."

Heinckel nodded. "Last time that horse called you, Maxie, I lost my sister-in-law's fiancé."

The short man shrugged again. "Nobody ever said Regan was no pushover."

"My sister-in-law still won't talk to me or my wife."

"That's one more favor you owe me."

Heinckel stared, almost without seeing, at the small man. Although he had made good money—big money—with Maxie, neither Heinckel nor any of his people could ever warm up to him. Maxie had come as a stranger two years before, speaking the strange language of the city, making veiled references to shadowy "principals" in Manhattan and Brooklyn, men who apparently shared his take without once laying their lives on the line, as Heinckel's people did. Nobody liked Maxie or the fact that he made little effort to keep his money and his interests here on the South Shore. But, nevertheless, the money was there to be earned. And somebody had to earn it. So . . .

Heinckel swabbed the bar in front of the short man. "How many of Regan's men will be gunning for us?"

"How the fuck would I know?"

Heinckel winced. "Don't get so mad. I just asked."

"I don't care what it takes to put Regan out of business. He's gotta learn he can't bring in booze over my beach. If it'll make you any happier," Maxie said. "I gotta crew waiting in Moriches on the cruiser. Two are ex-Marine machine gunners. They learned it chopping up greasers in Nicaragua. Good enough for you? If not, I can make out fine without your turdkickers."

"I'll try, Maxie, I'll try."

With no further ado, the short, thin man turned and walked past the knot of men at the radio and out of the bar. He strolled casually outside and glanced at the sky. The moon had begun to come up over the northeastern horizon but low-lying clouds scudded across it, driven by a sharp May wind.

He could hear the radio from inside the Dutchman's. A woman's voice was moaning, "No one here can love or understand me. Oh, what hard luck stories they all hand me. Pack up—"

Maxie's thin mouth split in a grin. He got behind the wheel of the open-sided Packard touring car and drove east toward Moriches. Beautiful moon, he thought. You could call it a perfect hijacker's moon.

Chapter 6

Harry Regan led the roan mare over the sand at the west end of Ocean Beach village, where no one lived. He struggled up over the crest of the dune, sand giving way beneath his boots, horse scrambling wildly behind him.

He led her along the flat stretch of sand at the back base of the dunes, out of the way of the wind, toward a boarded-up cottage. Harry stopped for a moment to listen to the night sounds, sorting them out for signals of danger. Then he tied the mare in the lee of the cottage and plodded on alone through the sand to where the lights of Goldie Fain's house shone.

He eased himself inside by a back door, shut it silently behind him, and immediately stood stock still. Goldie had company.

He listened for a while to the back and forth of the two voices, hers and a man's, his very deep and resonant. One of her actor buddies, Harry decided. He made a lot of noise as he advanced through the hall toward the front of the house.

"Who's there?" Goldie called. Her voice sounded panicky.

"Who the hell would it be at this hour, darlin'?"

"My God, Paul."

"Not Paul," Harry said, entering the living room.

She gave him one of her idiotic grins, her straw-blonde hair shining in the candlelight. "Harry, this is Paul. Paul Lachaise, Harry Regan."

Harry watched the thin man get very slowly to his feet and poke out his hand. " 'm drunk on y'r booze, Harrah," he mumbled.

Regan shook his hand rather ceremoniously, twice. "Seen you before, Lachaise."

"Yuh?" Lachaise slid sideways a step, then regained his balance.

"In London. At the Aldwich."

Harry watched the man's eyes narrow from a wide, rather wild diameter to reddish slits. "Sweet shit," Lachaise intoned, his diction suddenly improving, "you caught my immortal Hamlet?"

Harry nodded. "That would be, uh, four years ago?"

Lachaise picked up an empty glass, poured it halfway with Scotch, and handed it to Regan. "Srink," he commanded, his pronunciation softening again. "Srink zeeply, ol' fend."

Goldie gave him a disgusted look. "You'd do a swell Hamlet now, you falling-down unkdray umpchay."

Lachaise seemed to mind this. He turned reproach-fully to her, then to Harry, then to the sofa and sat down suddenly. "Can't seem t'do anything right tonight," he remarked mostly to himself.

Regan sat down next to him and sipped the whisky. "You did a terrible Hamlet," he began conversationally, "but it was catnip to the ladies. I never heard such soul-ful moaning at intermissions."

He grinned and turned to Goldie. "I made the mistake of taking this classy little limey number to the show. I mean, normally, the Bard is not for me, you understand. But she was a bug on Shakespeare, said she. I found out she was bugs on this gink here." He cocked his thumb at Lachaise.

"I had no idea you were a theatregoer," Goldie said. "You always seemed more like the stay-at-home type, if you know what I mean." She arched her plucked eye-brows at him.

"In England, four years ago, I was different from what I am on Fire Island tonight," Harry wiggled his eye-brows, "if you know what I mean."

"In a different line?" Goldie asked.

"Different everything. Even a different name."

She shrugged. "Oh, a different name. Ever hear of Gittel Feinberg? Me. And this one here, if I remember, started off his life of drunkenness as Pasquale Somethingorother, you know, Eyetralian."

"I'll have you know," Lachaise intoned mellifluously from his end of the sofa, "that my mother was a Creole belle of Old New Orleans born to the fair name of Lachaise."

"And your old man?"

He sketched a faint bow as he sat there. "Had I but known him, Miss Feinberg, I would now be able to put a proper handle to him. But, as the man says, I never had the pleasure." He looked at Harry and Goldie in turn. Regan was dismayed to see that Lachaise's eyes were brimming with tears.

"You're from New Orleans?" Regan asked, to distract him.

"Ah own the soft impeachment, suh."

"I never knew that," Goldie chimed in. "You don't sound it, honey."

"Ah have always sought to increaserate mah under-standeration of the pronuncitatiousness of you Northern gentlefolk."

Regan grinned at Lachaise. "You talk real good."

"My commandatoriosity of the maternalacious tongue undergoes intensificatory elevateration with deep simul-taneousness."

Goldie sat down on the wicker sofa between the two men. "You have to stop him when he starts this. It's like a fit. And if he won't stop, you have to paste him one in the mush."

"It wasn't too damned long ago," Lachaise retorted, in perfect control of his diction, "that you were upbraiding me for never wanting to discuss anything serious. Now,

47

when I begin to unveil some of the glories of really plush conversation, you balk."

"What kind of serious stuff?" Regan asked Goldie.

"The world." She gestured in a frustrated, meaningless way, as if she had the world, dripping wet, in a cheesecloth bag and was unsuccessfully trying to wring it out.

"This crazy world," Lachaise amended.

She turned to face Regan. "It's crazy, all right. You ought to know that better than anybody."

"Why me?"

"Because you've . . . oh, been everywhere and done everything."

"Have I?" Harry finished the whisky in his glass. "Sometimes a reputation like that is valuable. All sorts of rumors astir. The more unreal I am in most people's minds, the better I like it."

"Unreal," Lachaise echoed, "we are all."

He sighed and a tear fell from his eye, coursing down his cheek. "Everything's changing, Harry Regan. The whole world is changing. And when the changing is over, none of anything will be real."

"I think," Goldie muttered, "I'd better paste him in the mush."

"He's all right," Harry assured her.

"Depends on what you mean by all right," Lachaise suggested.

Regan stood up and went to the window. He stood with his back to the blackness outside. "I just dropped in to say hello," he said then. "I'll be on my way now."

Goldie made a face. "Stay a little?"

"We'll all talk serious," Lachaise put in. "We'll talk about Sacco and Vanzetti and Stalin and Trotsky and Diaz and Sacasa and Mussolini and—"

"Who the hell is Diaz?" Goldie asked.

Regan heaved a sigh. He had other things to do and he was beginning to be sorry he'd stopped by Goldie's. Normally, even with boyfriends on hand, she was good for a few laughs. And, God knew, you could always use a few laughs. But tonight she was in one of her cosmic moods. Occasionally, Harry knew, when the guilt of being nothing but a fluff-headed musical comedy star began to build deep in her Russian-Jewish soul and she started feeling keenly her betrayal of the learned piousness of her fathers, she would take a sudden, spurious interest in headlines. It usually lasted less than a week.

"One of the two current presidents of Nicaragua," he said, starting for the door. "A toady of the U.S. and a mining company stooge so, of course, he's the one we recognize."

"Don't leave yet. Who's Sacasa?"

"The other one. The one we landed six thousand Marines to finish off." Harry opened the front door and a sharp, tangy blast of salt air flew past him into the room.

"Close the door!" Goldie howled. "It's freezing."

Harry stared at the night, then glanced at his watch. He shivered. He had a few minutes to spare, but only a few. He closed the door and refilled his glass.

"You're a political man," Lachaise said suddenly. He

had been huddled at his end of the wicker sofa, staring into his whisky. His voice sounded neither drunk nor mock-mellifluous but only tired.

"Not I."

"For a second there you sounded political."

"The only politics that ever interested me," Harry said, sitting on a chair across from Lachaise and Goldie, "were the politics of Ireland. And them not too much any more."

"Ireland?" Lachaise's voice drooped. "How the hell could anybody keep track of Irish politics?"

Harry shrugged. "It can be done, if you've a mind. But I'm not talking about who's agin who and who's made a coalition with what and all that day-to-day eye-wash that goes by the name of Irish politics. I'm talking about all of us and the English."

"I thought," Goldie piped up, "the Irish hated the English."

"That they do, girl. Devoutly." Harry finished his whisky. Then he held up the empty glass. "This is the only decent thing the English ever produced. And 'twas the Scots did it for 'em."

Lachaise cleared his throat and began to sing a thin, keening song meant for a march but softened, as he sang it, to a dirge.

"I'll sing you a song, a soldier's song, with cheering, rousing chorus.

As 'round the blazing fire we throng, the starry heavens o'er us."

Harry's higher voice joined in, trying to pump some

rhythm into the wailing tune. They continued singing together:

"Impatient for the coming fight

And as we await the morning light,

Here in the stillness of the night

We will chant a soldier's song."

"Ah, it's all wrong, man," Harry cut in. "It's a march and you're making a wake of it. Where did you learn to sing it that way?"

Lachaise grinned at him. "In England, of course."

Harry laughed. "If you'll pardon me, your rhythm is off. Let me teach you a song with a real swing to it. No fake heroics, just a pure song of pure hate. Are you game?"

"Me too?" Goldie asked.

"Both of yez. Now, you beat out the tempo for me like this." Harry began to slap his knee. "Dum-di-di-dum, di-di-dum-dum-dum," he said. "Like a jig." He waited till they had gotten together and steady. Then he began the *recitavo* in a low, tense voice:

"They came on the promise of money. Blood money. They came from the prisons of Dartmoor and Peterhead, the dregs of English perversion and crime. They came to murder, to torture and to maim. We called them the Black and Tan and black were their hearts and black is the hell to which they go. For the Black and Tan reckoned without the boys of Barry's Flying Column."

He stopped for a moment and watched his two drummer boys, one perhaps the best known Shakespearean leading man in a decade, the other a comedienne of some renown. They were staring raptly at him as their hands beat out the jiglike tattoo Harry Regan required for the song.

When he began to sing, the tune was a warped, amodal line, half minor, half major, that twisted around the notes with a life of its own, slipping into the cracks between half tones like an Arab chant.

"From east to west, from north to south,
    They tried to hunt the column out;
    But the Tans were forced to go without
    The boys of Barry's Column.
    Lloyd George may have some wily tricks
    On how the volunteers to fix,
    But all his Black and Tans go sick
    To think of Barry's Column.
    Oh, but isn't it grand to see the Tommies and the R.A.C.,
    Black and Tans and sailors flee
    Away from Barry's Column."

He grinned at his two drummers and encouraged them to pick up the beat slightly for the next chorus.

"This prison scum in brown and black
    No tanks or war equipment lack
    From o'er the sea they'll ne'er get back
    At the boys of Barry's Column.
    They stopped to rest for just a spell;
    Some hand grenades upon them fell.
    'Here, share them out among yourselves!'
    Said the boys of Barry's Column."

As he sang the refrain, Harry urged them to join him. Goldie had learned it already and her funny voice, partly hoarse and partly speaking rather than singing, fitted in around Harry's high baritone.

"Along the lonely road they wind,
Armed in front and armed behind.
'We're sorry, but that bridge was mined,'
By the boys of Barry's Column.
From prison cells they came to stay
And wipe our Irish boys away.
But, oh, their lovely holiday
Was spoiled by Barry's Column.
Oh, but isn't it grand to see the Tommies and the R.A.C.,
Black and Tans and sailors flee
From the boys of Barry's Column."

Harry sighed and quieted his percussion section. "A darlin' hymn of hate," he said, getting to his feet. "And now, having spread sunshine, I must be on me merry way."

"My God, Harry," Goldie said. "They really hate the English, don't they?"

Regan nodded. He felt the seawind in his face as he opened the door again. "I shouldn't wonder," he said, half in and half out of the house, "If the Nicaraguans don't feel the same way about us."

He slammed the door tight shut behind him and slid off down the back of the dune, scrambling through sand to reach the path at the bottom that led toward where he had tethered the mare.

Amazing, he thought, as he plodded toward the far end of the village, that two people like that could go so far in the performing arts with such rotten senses of rhythm.

Some have seen in this magnificent flight an impious flaunting of the Deity's supremacy. But they forget that God chooses his own instruments. It is no accident that an American has been chosen. The Supreme Being is showing us unmistakably His own way toward a new supremacy on Earth of His word. A day is dawning when His hegemony will be militantly advanced by Americans winging courageously across the planet, thrusting His flaming torch of truth into the dark corners of the ignorant heathen, the godless socialist and the corrupt idolater.

(Rev.) Emily Parkinson Hayes

(as quoted in the
San Francisco *Chronicle*,
May 30, 1927)

Chapter 7

"Pay some attention," the old man said.

There was a slight edge to his voice because the younger man, hardly in his twenties, had long ago lost interest in the radio equipment and was standing at the tall window of the Second Avenue tenement staring five floors down at the corner of 86th Street.

A fight had just broken out there between the *Daily News* driver and the driver for the *Mirror*. They had both delivered their extra editions, each black with type blazoning Lindbergh's departure, and they had both retired to Groark's speak, hidden back behind its cigar, newspaper, and soda fountain façade. After a few belts of Groark's gargle, mostly homemade over in Jersey by ignorant Italian labor, the two drivers had been asked to transfer their hostilities to the public pavement and stop disturbing Groark's clientele with their threats and inelegant cursing.

"Are y'for God's sake even listening at all?" the old man snarled.

The younger turned from the window. "I haven't heard a thing to listen to for the last five minutes, you blathering old ninny."

The old man bared his teeth, displaying several brownish gaps. "What kind of piss-in-the-pants, wet-behind-the-ears bully boy have they sent me this time? Fair out of their minds they must be in Dublin to pay passage for the likes of you, y'lousy scut."

The younger man made a resigned face and sat down backwards on a bentwood chair, facing the radio. "I've so far followed all your gassing, old man. We get the signal from Heaney in Sheepshead Bay after he gets it from the ship. He gets it the same time Harry Regan does. Am I right so far?"

"So far," the old man admitted grudgingly.

"And then, quick as spite, we relay the signal to Clarke over in Corona, where the garage is, and he starts the trucks rolling. What I don't understand is this." He hitched himself closer to the radio. "I've been studying a map of this city of New York and as far as I can tell Heaney is a lot closer to Corona than we are."

"But not higher. The man's at sea level and the radio waves won't carry to Corona without a lot more power."

"Then let Heaney get more power."

"For the government to listen to and hear? If there is one thing I don't need from Dublin, it's them sending me one more fool." The old man gave his companion a disgusted look. "Being higher here, we get Heaney's message at a lower power and relay it to Clarke at a lower power without letting half the Federal agents along the East Coast know what the hell we're about. Is that clear enough for you?"

The young man shrugged. "What I don't understand is all the hocus-pocus. Why in hell can't the likes of Harry Regan set up his own trucks? The way you talk of him, he's half a genius and half a devil as it is."

The older man nodded. " 'Twas Harry set up the whole apparatus, as he calls it. Everything, from start to finish. We handled it first by telephone, but Harry said it wasn't secure and beside, this was the twentieth century and, by God, he'd have us using radios or go out of business entirely. A very forward-looking man, Harry Regan."

"There were Regans in County Mayo," the young man mused.

"Not likely the same. This Regan was born in the Park Slope section of Brooklyn. Where his old man and woman came from is beyond me."

The younger man frowned. "And the movement leaves leadership in the hands of a Yankee? They didn't tell me none of this when they sent me over here."

"Why the hell should they?" the old man demanded. "Who the hell are you, may I ask, to know the movement's inner workings? It's enough to know the signal procedure. You'd never understand Harry Regan in a million years, boy, and don't even try."

"If my freedom and my life depend on him," the

younger man said in a slow, mulish way, "then I'd god-damned better be knowing something about the man."

"A place for everything," the old man said, "and everything in its place. That's one of Harry's ideas. First show me you know your signals. Then maybe I'll tell you a little more about Harry Regan."

The mulish look deepened on the younger man's face. He sighed resignedly. "We use the old Morse," he began in a deliberately dull singsong monotone. "We don't use the International Morse because it's what the Coast Guard expects. We use letters by shape, not position or meaning. We use their small-letter shape, not capitals. We use b and d and p interchangeably because they all have the shape of the path of a ship reaching a point and then circling till further orders are received. C and j are also interchangeable and have the shape of a 180 degree turnaround. The small h is an interception signal. It has the shape of one ship on course while the other curves into it from starboard. The small i is a dump signal, like something being dropped overboard. The small k is a rendezvous, having the shape of a straight course with . . ."

The young man's voice droned on. Outside the window on the windy May night, voices raised in anger carried a great distance. ". . . x is a clear meeting, a crossing of two lines. Y is a fast split-off of a launch." The singsong ended. "Tell me about Regan."

The old man sniffed. He picked up a dark cherrywood pipe and began cramming blackish tobacco into its small bowl. "Let me ask you something first, boy. How old are you now? Maybe twenty?"

The younger man's face darkened. "Nineteen. What's it to do with Harry Regan?"

"Nothing, nothing. Tell me one thing more before I try to paint the picture for you. Are you after being a virgin still?"

Chapter 8

Harry Regan hunched over the round oak table in the kitchen of the Purvis house just east of Point O' Woods, where the Sunken Forest began. Ellen Purvis had given him a mug of black coffee to drink while her husband went out to the shed to get the ammo box Harry kept there. Harry laced his fingers around the clean, hot china and hugged it to his breast. The wind had put a chill in him as he had galloped up and down the beach. He had covered the length of it from the inlet to far past Cherry Grove. Everyone he could count on had been alerted. Now it was time for him and Jim Purvis to look to the boats.

Harry grinned up at Ellen. Her hair, blonde almost to whiteness, shimmered in the pale rays of the oil lamp hanging over the table. "Any of that Bushmill's left?"

Ellen gave him a conspirator's smile. She produced a square bottle of Irish whiskey and poured a full dollop into Harry's coffee.

Harry took a long sip and grinned again at her. He brushed the reddish hair off his forehead and then, with a downward motion of the same hand, circled Ellen's waist and squeezed. "How is it keeping, darlin'?" he asked, slipping into a brogue. "Is it still hiding away in there, the wee blonde thing?"

She bent down and nipped at his ear lobe, then moved off toward the stove as they heard Purvis's footsteps on the back deck of the house. "It's still a little sore after last week," she whispered, "if it makes the slightest difference to you."

"Here," Purvis grunted, shoving open the door, his hands grasping the rope handle at each end of the metal-bound Springfield case Harry used for ammo. It had once been packed with a half-dozen rifles in Cosmolene. Now it was filled with loose 9 mm. cartridges for the Luger Parabellum and eight of the peculiar metal "snail" magazines Harry had bought from a German sailor in Havana three years before, during the Machado campaign. The magazines held 32 shells each in a spiral configuration that clipped into the left side of the automatic. When they didn't jam they gave Harry a firepower superior to any handgun the Coast Guard could muster. After using all of them, Harry knew the four magazines that were prone to jamming and the four that worked smoothly. It was these he picked out of the case now and lined up on the round oak table. He began feeding 9 mm. shells into the magazines.

"Almost ten o'clock," Ellen Purvis said. "Shouldn't you get moving?"

Harry made a face as he looked up at Purvis. "Your boys waiting at the dock in Saltaire?"

"There and Kismet."

"I'll give you a ten-minute start. It wouldn't look too good for both of us to go gunning down the bay full throttle at this hour."

Purvis glanced at his wife. His face went blank. "We'll rendezvous off Kismet at eleven. Where's your bunch meeting?"

Harry started loading a second magazine. "Various private places, Jimmy. It wouldn't do to have crews lining up on every dock along the bay, now would it."

"I guess not." Purvis started to leave, then stopped. He seemed unable to think of what he had it in mind to say. Harry Regan watched his mouth frame and reframe several words.

"Spit it out, Jim."

"Nothing. See you at eleven."

Purvis left without saying good-bye to Ellen or Harry. After a moment they heard the inboard engines of his boat sputter and catch, then roar into life as he cast off and pulled away into the bay. Harry got up and stared out the rear window. Satisfied, he sat down and began loading the third magazine.

Ellen's long, thin tongue darted into his ear. "How much good can we do in ten minutes?" she whispered, the breath tickling the inner hairs of his ear.

He put down the metal magazine, turned slightly in his chair, and bit her lower lip softly. "Not a hell of a lot, darlin'. How would you like to ship along tonight in my boat? Between times I'd hop down in the cabin and give you a few inches where it'd do the most good."

"You're like a stud horse," she said. "You're like an animal. You'd do it anywhere. To anybody. Wouldn't you?"

Harry shook his head slowly. "Only to pretty women like you."

"And Maeve Curran. And the Horvath girl in Center Moriches. And Goldie Fain in Ocean Beach. And that black-haired daughter of Old Man Phillips. And every female from here to Montauk Point for all I know."

Harry's eyes lost their sparkle. "You don't understand me at all, do you, Ellen?"

"I understand I'm cheating on a pretty decent man for the pleasure of a few tickles up the behind from you."

"Christ, blondes always were great moralizers."

"Me moralize?" Ellen smiled grimly. "You don't hear me sending you away, do you?" She broke away from Harry and went to look at herself in the mirror next to the water pump on the sink. She touched her longish hair. "Next week I'm going to that beauty shop in Patchogue. I'm going to get this mess bobbed to an inch of its life. I'll stay overnight with a girl friend. At the Drover's Hotel there. Next Thursday?"

There was a longish pause. "I wouldn't want to be putting any tremendous strain on your immortal soul, darlin'," Harry said then. "Why don't we just forget it?" He began loading the last magazine.

Ellen turned to face him. "Please."

He shrugged as he pressed the bullets one after another into the snail-shell case. "I'm not a great one for such grand advance planning. To my mind it sort of takes the edge off the whole thing, Ellen. I mean, here we are, right now. I'm ready and you're willing. Why do we have to start putting it on the calendar and planning ahead like a pair of bankers or what-have-you?"

"Will you stop playing with that?" she burst out.

Harry put down the magazine. "Edgy tonight?"

"Very. Got a cigarette?"

He handed her one and held the match for her. "You want to be careful Jim doesn't find out you smoke. Either."

"Don't razz me, Harry."

"Or drink, for that matter." He sighed and resumed loading the magazine. "What a great number of secrets you have, Ellen. You've got your life just about as complicated as you can get it, haven't you?"

"Thanks to you."

"I'm only one of the secrets."

She came back and sat down on Harry's lap. "Kiss me."

He shoved the last cartridge in the magazine. "Ten minutes are up, darlin'. Time for young Harry to be on his way."

"I'm sorry I—"

"So am I," he cut in. "Now let me be up and doing. It's going to be a long night."

She got to her feet as he did and watched him pack

the loaded magazines in a khaki-colored canvas musette bag with rusty metal fittings. Harry slung the strap over his shoulder and let the heavy bag hang down behind him against the small of his back.

"I suppose," Ellen mused as she watched him adjust the strap slightly, "you'd rather do this kind of thing than spend the night at the Drover's Hotel."

"A place for everything and everything in its place," Harry said. "I may be there next Thursday and then again I may be laid out on view at Hanratty's Funeral Home in Speonk."

"Promise you'll meet me?"

"I may."

"You won't regret it, Harry. None of these other women know half what I do."

He frowned thoughtfully. After a moment he sat down on the chair again. He gestured to her and she sat down in his lap, her skirts spread out around her. She was facing him with a leg dangling on either side. Harry fumbled briefly beneath her dress. Now her thigh muscles flexed and tightened as he entered her from beneath.

Her arms went around him and her mouth was at his ear again. Their movements were minimal. In this position even a slight shift could produce a full sensation. Someone watching them would probably not have known that anything more than an embrace was happening.

The change in angle of thrust inflamed Harry's entire groin. Nerve endings were being rasped that were usually only stroked. Ellen's breath in his ear seemed to ignite the canals leading into his brain. She was moaning now, a sound like a wet finger on a glass. Her vulva had grown suddenly tighter as she neared climax. The strange pressures and frictions drove Harry closer to the edge of orgasm. He could hear her breathing quicken in a series of rising gasps. He tensed, trying to outwait her. Suddenly the slight back and forth movement of her pelvis stopped. She seemed to freeze for a moment. Then her teeth sank into Harry's earlobe as she reached climax with a faint inward thrust. Pain shot through Harry's head. He jammed up into her with a brutal ramming movement he knew would hurt her. As she began to cry out, he came in a single hard upthrust.

They sat motionless for a long moment. Harry felt his ear and looked at the blood on his fingers. "Bitch."

"You love it."

"Vampire bitch. And you want a night of it at the Drover's? Not likely."

"You'll be there."

He stood up without warning, toppling her off his lap. She grabbed at his arm and managed to stand up. "Always the gentleman, Harry."

He started for the door, then seemed to change his mind. "Of all the people in this world who don't know Harry Regan, I would say your name comes near the top of the list. Darlin'," he added mockingly.

"What's to know? The cock that walks like a man."

"Purvis told me once you'd taken a year of college. Is that true?"

"What if it is?"

Harry found himself getting angry, something he never did with a woman. "Is that where you got your profound insights into my life?" He started for the door again. "Save your money Thursday, Ellen. Forget the Drover's Hotel."

"What are you besides a hooligan, rum-running stud? What are you pretending to be," she asked, "some kind of Robin Hood? Am I supposed to see that underneath what I see there's a fine man, a real hero? Instead of an over-grown baby boy playing cops and robbers when he ought to be settling down to a man's life?" She took a breath and it came out shaking with rage. "Am I supposed to pretend that you're something special, Harry? Because other than that cock of yours, you aren't worth the powder the Coast Guard will take to blow you to hell."

He started to snap an answer, then halted. His teeth showed in a malicious grin. "Don't knock the cock, darlin'. It gave you many a fine moment."

Ellen's mouth opened. But instead of speaking, she began to laugh. "God Almighty, I can't even stay mad at you, you idiot."

She stood in the doorway as he started off down the walk to the private dock. "Maybe you are something special at that," she called after him.

"No maybes about it. Darlin'!"

Chapter 9

Lt. Ashley got up slowly from his bunk bed, every mid-riff muscle aching, and walked with the shaky dignity of an elderly man to the mirror on the far wall of his room. He avoided his small blue eyes as he smoothed back the short, damp blonde hair from both sides of his center part. Then he rebuttoned his collar and slid the knot of his tie up tight against his throat until he almost gagged.

He was drunk. He knew it and he worried that every-one else would know it. But, in another part of his mind, he was well aware that he had been this drunk before without anyone noticing his condition.

Ashley frowned at one collar point, seeing that he had gotten it damp during the past hour. But whether the dampness was sweat or spit or Scotch, he had no idea. The uncertainty bothered him. He surrendered to the need to look into his own eyes, trying to read in them some sign that he would be all right, or was going insane, or something else, something concrete and know-able.

Of all the many things in the world Ashley hated, being uncertain was the worst. He literally could not stand un-certainty. It didn't just unnerve him, it seemed actually to unjoint, unstring, and lay him out in separate pieces, like fowl ready for broiling.

He was very much aware of this particular problem, but knowing how he felt seemed to have no good effect on the problem. In fact, Ashley realized now as he watched himself in the mirror, knowing what disturbed him—the very act of feeling disturbed—seemed to worsen the feeling. He felt like a dog chasing his own tail. The faster he turned, the more excited and upset he grew.

Surely, Ashley thought now, surely there had to be some kind of peace for him somewhere in the world.

He had been sure, at one point, that the Coast Guard was the right place for him. Everything was preordained, classified, sealed off in compartments, and the distinctions strictly enforced. One knew, from day to day and year to year, what the future would be. It was very much like working for any other big organization—the Post Office or an insurance company or the Treasury Department—in that all one really had to do to keep relatively safe and sure of the future was to do one's own job and shut up.

Ashley grimaced at his face in the mirror. This was another of the lies he had been uncovering lately. There didn't seem to be anything more certain about being in the Coast Guard than being anywhere else in this crazy world. Everything was changing. People were flying airplanes across the Atlantic, Harry Regan was punching huge holes in the coastal security line, Chief Heydt was mocking Ashley in his hidden, nasty way, headquarters was paying no attention to requests, his mother . . .

He turned from the mirror and looked around for his jacket. He had thrown it carelessly across the room, probably during the heat of the colitis attack, and now it would be wrinkled. He was smoothing it out when Ensign Jorgensen knocked.

"Lieutenant Ashley, sir?"

Ashley stood up straighter before turning around to meet him. He wondered whether the younger man would know what the faint odor in the room was. Jorgensen seemed almost too innocent to know what liquor was, let alone how it smelled, but one couldn't be too careful.

"How was the patrol, Mister?"

Jorgensen nodded several times, enthusiastically. "Tremendous, sir. I don't know if you've had a chance to check the moon, sir, but she's riding behind scud. Now you see her, now you don't. And it's quite a sight, let me tell you."

"Why don't you try telling me what your patrol discovered, Mister."

Ashley's words were absolutely devoid of coloring. It was high time he took some of the spontaneity and spunk out of Jorgensen, for the boy's own good. He wasn't taking his responsibilities seriously. He kept treating the nighttime picket-duty patrols as some kind of Sea Scout exercise, complete with nature-guide commentaries.

"Yes, sir." Jorgensen's normally ruddy face, with its high cheekbones, turned a brick red. His eyes crawled sideways, as if seeking possible escape hatches from the immense cauldron into which his stupidity had plunged him.

"You'll learn," Ashley remarked, letting his voice get louder and surer. "These patrols are serious business, Mister. You'll learn just how serious some night when you run across a rum boat that shoots first, instead of taking to its heels."

"Yes, sir."

"The only thing that's made it seem such a picnic to you," Ashley continued in a confident bellow, "is that these rum boys are all cowards. They'd rather turn and run than stand and fight. But don't make any mistake; they can give you plenty of trouble when you start crowding them."

"Yes, sir."

"All right."

"Yes, sir."

"Let's take a look at the charts while you make your report."

"Yes, sir."

Ashley led the way along a narrow hallway to another room. He pulled down a large-scale map of the entire barrier beach configuration from its beginnings in the Coney Island area of Brooklyn and the Rockaways through Long Beach and along Jones and Captree to Fire Island itself, leading eastward all the time to the Hamptons and, past Shinnecock Bay, to where it joined the mainland of the island at Southampton.

"We'll use the big map first. Then we'll zero in on the area map when I start asking you more specific questions."

"Yes, sir." Jorgensen's Adam's apple bobbed twice in anticipation of the more specific questions.

"All right, Mister. Report."

"Yes, sir."

Ashley approved of the waver in Jorgensen's voice. While it simply wasn't possible to teach a Chief like Heydt, it was superbly easy to keep an officer like this boy hopping with anxiety. All in all, Ashley decided, he'd do better to keep his distance from the shifty, corrupt enlisted men and concentrate on officers like Jorgensen, for their own good.

The younger man swallowed again. "Patrol commenced at sundown, approximately eighteen-thirty hours, from Coast Guard bay pier and proceeded due west through Fire Island Inlet approximately five miles into open sea off Democrat Point." Jorgensen's voice was gaining confidence as he buried himself in the inane trivia of the report.

"Patrol then commenced a zigzag sweep in directions northeast and southeast, allowing approximately fifteen minutes per tack, with a general easterly bearing until reaching a point approximately four miles offshore from the Narrow Bay area off Smith Point and Mastic."

Jorgensen paused to take a breath and Ashley could see what he imagined was a faint gleam of self-satisfaction at having gotten off the preliminary report without a mistake.

"My, but we're pleased with ourselves, aren't we, Mister?" he barked. "All you've told me is how you circled from the bay around the point into the ocean. Let's get down to specifics, if it isn't too much trouble."

"Yes, sir." Ashley watched the Adam's apple bob twice.

"Patrol encountered three fishing trawlers running seines in a lane approximately six miles offshore Fire Island from approximately Ocean Beach approximately five miles to approximately Cherry Grove. Said trawlers appeared to be common forty-foot coal-burning trawlers of the South Bay Fishing Corporation in their normal nighttime positions and duty."

Jorgensen's eyes twitched sideways to note any effect of the report on Ashley. He was quickly rewarded.

"You're great with those approximately's and appeared-to-be's, aren't you, Mister? How about some hard facts? Shoot."

"Yes, sir. At twenty-forty-five hours, patrol raised an unidentified vessel about ten miles offshore Cherry Grove. Vessel was in process of turning when patrol raised her. Before patrol could give chase vessel headed further out to sea beyond twelve-mile line. Patrol held to picket-mission pattern and continued eastward sweep. On return sweep at approximately twenty-two hundred hours, patrol raised similar vessel in roughly the same location. Once again it was in the process of turning out to sea, which maneuver it completed and disappeared beyond the limit. Patrol—"

"Is full of shit," Ashley interrupted.

"Sir?"

"Any numbskull knows what happened. Their lookouts were better than yours, Mister. They were spotting you long before you were spotting them. And they were already heading out to sea by the time you made them. Isn't that just beautiful, Mister? Any common thief and criminal in the rum fleet has better eyes than the pick of the United States Coast Guard?"

Jorgensen's lips twisted as they framed several phrases. Ashley got ready to shoot down any form of apology. Then: "N-no excuse, sir."

Ashley smiled slightly. "That, Mister, is the only correct answer you have left. There's no excuse in the world for what happened."

"Sir?"

"Yes?"

"Begging the Lieutenant's pardon, sir, but if we had spotted them first and given chase, it's my opinion we wouldn't have been able to overhaul them before they were well beyond the twelve-mile line." The boy's eyes darted furiously around the room, as if frightened to death of the boldness of the words.

Ashley paused for a moment. It was easy enough to continue teaching Jorgensen, he reflected, but there was no more point to it, really. The lesson had been learned and arguing with him on nit-picking points like who could overhaul what didn't help matters a great deal. But there was time for one more point.

"That may or may not be so, Mister," Ashley said then. "It's not a question either of us can answer, can we? Because you didn't give chase, did you? Because they were already outmaneuvering you, weren't they? So the question's academic."

"But, sir?"

"Yes?"

"For the future, sir, so I can be guided accordingly, when we're that close to the limit line, is there any point in giving chase? Even when we spot them first?"

"Is there any point?" Ashley let the question ring into the silence between them. "What are you asking me, Mister? If we don't give chase to a criminal when we see him, is there any point in anything we stand for?"

"Sir, I didn't quite mean it that—"

"It doesn't matter if he's five feet inside the line, Mister." Ashley's voice had started to boom and he felt himself gripped by his words. It was as if there were something superior inside him speaking, a something he could see and hear that wasn't himself, but was far above himself.

"It doesn't matter whether he's got a faster craft than we have, either," Ashley shouted. "Nor that his engines are newer. Nor that, goddamn it to hell, he bought them as surplus from the same Uncle Sam who pays us to hunt him down. Nor that those Liberty engines of his can turn out higher revs than any of our clunkers. Nor that he burns better grade fuel than we get. Nor that his radio equipment sparks rings around ours. Nor that he's transmitting and receiving on wavelengths we don't even have. Nor that half the population of Long Island and New York is in cahoots with him. Nor that the other half is busy buying his stuff to make the whole thing possible. Nor that we're undermanned and underequipped. None of that whole chickenshit mess means anything, Mister. What matters is that, by Christ, when you see the bastard, you give chase. Hear me?" he shouted. "You give chase!"

Jorgensen's eyes were wide. He seemed to be staring into a tremendous heat that made his eyes water, some gigantic furnace whose door he had accidentally swung open.

"No matter what, Mister!" Ashley yelled, his voice filling the room with a passion that shocked even him as he heard it. "You listen real good. There's a right in this world and there's a wrong. And that's that, Mister. Right is right and wrong is wrong."

Ashley heard a slight sound behind him and whirled, hand rising, as if to ward off a blow.

Chief Heydt stood in the doorway, eyes motionless as he observed Ashley. "Permission to report, sir."

"Report." Ashley's voice sounded hoarse and as shaken now as Jorgensen's had a few minutes before. "Snap it up, Heydt."

"Sir." Heydt paused very deliberately. "We've monitored a signal from the direction of Long Cove to the east. Before we could get a full fix on it the signal failed.

Apparently they're trying to launch pickup craft through the surf and having a rough time."

Ashley's breathing slowed. "That's pretty goddamned peculiar, Chief."

"My feeling, sir. Thought you should know."

"How can they expect to launch craft of any size at all through the surf?"

"No idea, sir."

"What gave you the idea they were trying such a maneuver?"

Heydt's eyebrows lifted a fraction of an inch. "The signal, sir. It was rough and kind of rushed. But they were calling for more men because the wind had turned. At least that's what I made of it."

"What sense does Spanier make of it?"

"He wasn't there, sir. I was on the board alone."

"So that you could have misheard or misinterpreted the signals as easily as not," Ashley pounced. Immediately he wished he had not. He knew it did him no good to try this with Heydt. The man was unteachable.

"Perfectly possible, sir," Heydt agreed, his glance moving to a point slightly above Ashley's head.

"All right. Back to duty. I'll discuss it with you later."

"Sir." Heydt about-faced and left.

There was a long moment of silence between the two officers, which Jorgensen broke with a tentative: "Sir, I think the Chief was a little—"

"That'll do, Mister," Ashley cut in. "You've got a post, too. Let's get back to it on the double."

"Yes, sir."

Chapter 10

Outside the shack the wind roved from side to side, veering like a hound on a scent. Maeve had fallen asleep in the rocker with a mug half full of cold tea in her hands. The keening of the wind snapped her awake and she sat up, sloshing the dark brown liquid onto her cardigan. She cursed and went to the sink.

Thoroughly chilled now, she worked the handle of the pump and sent a thin spout of fresh water over a washrag. She rubbed at the stain. Tea that strong, she knew, could stain for good and all. What was it her mother used on tea stains? Lemon juice? Yes, and leave it in the sun a day or so.

She poured fresh tea, sipped it, and found it lukewarm. She made a face, set the mug down on the sink, and paced restlessly about the cabin. Harry hadn't even started out to sea yet, most likely, or was just about to. The night hadn't really begun for him and here she was falling asleep in her rocking chair like an old woman.

Funny. She would believe her mother about tea stains, but not about Harry. He was the Antichrist, her mother had told her. He was Satan himself. And all he was was a poor, bloody soul whom nobody knew except Maeve. She yawned. Her eyes felt puffy with sleep. She yawned and immediately yawned again.

Maeve stood by the bed for a moment, trying to remember what she had been searching her memory for when she'd first fallen asleep. She yawned a fourth time. Then she undressed, blew out the kerosene lamp, and slid under the dampish sheets. Her legs prickled with gooseflesh. God, how she needed Harry's hot, bony body around and over her.

In the darkness now the wind seemed louder, more insistent. Maeve listened to it with her eyes open for a long time. Then she closed her eyes and let drowsiness creep over her. Poor bloody soul, she thought. And if I'm the only one in the world who understands him, what cold comfort for such a lovely man to be so ill-understood.

Under the sheet and the heavy comforters her body grew warmer. Her thoughts began to slide about hazily, losing their connections with one another. The smell was the first thing she noticed in a vision that was half dream and half memory.

It was a small thatched cottage. The slanty upper story was an attic reached by a ladder. The attic held some old furniture, a few dozen rounds of .38 cartridges, two Webley revolvers, and two men, one of them Harry Regan.

Now she placed the smell. In the June heat, the acrid

stench of the mildewed thatch was almost overpowering. Harry was reading a Dublin newspaper. The other man had no name. He and Harry had worked as a team for several months now and considered themselves as close as brothers. He had saved Harry's life once or twice and Harry had saved his as often or more. The man lay on his back now and snored very lightly as he slept.

The newspaper told Harry it was all over. It told him he had no more business hiding out in attics. It said the terrible three-month civil war De Valera and the Republican Society had waged against Mick Collins and the Dáil Éireann was over, or should be.

Dev's holy war to keep the Irish from licking Lloyd George's boots was over. It smelled of mildewed death, rotting in the June heat.

Harry Regan rolled on his back and stared at the thatch over him. It had all seemed so easy after the Tans had been withdrawn. In the election that followed, the Sinn Fein had won almost every seat. The conferences with Lloyd George had begun. Dev had rejected the offer of Dominion status. Ireland could not be free as part of Great Britain. And then the second round of negotiations had begun, but without Dev.

The rest was too recent to have lost its sting. Not even six months before, with Griffith and Mick Collins doing the treatying, Ireland had joined the Dominion as an abortion called the Irish Free State. Free!

Sold down the river by Mick himself, and Griffith, father of the Sinn Fein. And, worst of all, ignoring Dev's pleading, the Dáil itself ratifying the sell-out treaty. What could a man do but join Dev in a new guerrilla war, the Republicans against the cowards who had sworn an oath of loyalty to the King?

Now even that was finished. The Dublin paper said so. Elections had been held. The Collins forces had clearly defeated Dev at the polls. So be it. The gutless Irish wanted to wallow under the heel of the same treacherous British who had starved and murdered them for eight hundred years. So be it. Ireland, farewell.

Harry opened the trap door. The other man stirred. "Where to, lad?"

Maeve stirred in her sleep. She could taste the rancid mildew. She could see the look on his brother-in-arms's face as Harry told him he was leaving the movement, going back to the States. She could see his comrade raise the Webley and point its long barrel at Harry's heart.

She awoke in a rush of anxiety, sitting up in bed, her face flushed with the dream. Had she made it up? He must have told it to her. It was Harry's dream, not hers. She had never been inside a thatched cottage in her life.

But the stink of the mildew seemed to choke her. She got out of bed and ran on bare feet to the window. Clouds blotted out the moon. There was nothing to see outside but black night. The wind moaned around a corner of the shack and the pane of glass beneath her fingers trembled.

Then it all came back to her, the memory and Harry's telling of it. They'd made love through a whole afternoon and evening, finishing almost a fifth of Dewar's between them. Long past midnight, not really knowing where she was, floating happily, she had awakened alone in the bed. Naked, Harry stood at the window, staring out at the night just as she stood now.

The black dog was on him. He was remembering the sad old dreams of a perfect mankind. The priest's dream of salvation had risen in his throat like vomit.

". . . and I said he was crazy," he told Maeve, his voice low and hurried. "I said to put away the Webley, damned fool. And his first shot went wide so I leaped on him. We were like lovers, me on top of him, us thrashing about on that stinking attic floor. The Webley went off again before I twisted it out of his hand, but the slug went wild. I had both hands on his throat. He heaved like a bitch in heat. Under my fingers, his blood pumped through the big artery. I could feel him trying to swallow, to breathe, to stay alive. Red snakes burst out in the corners of his eyes. His face was purple. My hands were locked into his throat. When he died it was like a woman coming in one immense spasm. I left him to rot in that airless place. I squeezed the life out of him and I ran."

Maeve turned away from the window. She got slowly back into bed. The sheets received her like a damp shroud. She stretched out straight, arms crossed over her breasts. Her fine black hair lay spread about her on the pillow.

No dream. Harry's nightmare in life had come back to her in sleep. The brother-in-arms had died between his fingers and with him the whole priest's dream had died, too.

Chapter 11

Harry Regan squinted through the cold salt spray streaming past his face. He had just navigated through the channel between Fire Island Beach proper and the small chunks of land in Great South Bay variously known as the Fire Islands or the Penny Islands. Now he could make out the low-lying shape of another bit of land, Sexton Island, over his port bow.

The 32-foot boat lay as close to the water as Harry could keep her. He had found the *Deirdre* a year ago in a ship chandler's yard in Babylon, her scuppers awash. She had been built of thick oak planks some time in the 1880's as a centerboard sailboat with a long, peaky bow and sprit. Harry had rescued her for $20 and had himself installed twin four-cylinder Ford motors, ransacked from dilapidated Model T's at a nearby yard. He had brought the motors back to Brooklyn to a garage run by a friend, who had cut down their cylinder blocks to increase compression and had added a primitive type of blower-super-charger, hidden under the manifold to avoid detection. These innocent-seeming motors could drive the *Deirdre's* roomy hulk at a cruising speed of fifteen miles per hour and Harry could coax another five or six out of the craft with a judicious application of methyl alcohol in the fuel lines. The *Deirdre* most resembled a tired, waddling Great South Bay clam boat, which was the effect Harry had wanted to achieve.

He crouched now below her cockpit coaming and wondered how long the scud would keep the moon hidden. This was the first of the difficult passages in a night's adventure, slipping unobserved through the inlet to the Atlantic past the Coast Guard station.

Harry cut the engines to idling speed and gave cautious hand signals to the boat following him. The signal was passed back from boat to boat until the last of the seven craft had cut its engines. His eyes free of spray now, Harry stared up at the place in the sky where the moon would be.

The bay bucked and swelled under the *Deirdre*. A wind of well past 20 knots had kept the shallow water turbulent all through the tricky business of picking up crews and boats along ten miles of bay front. Harry watched the faintly whitish area of scud that hid the moon. The area seemed to extend, relatively unbroken, for a few miles to the windward of the moon's apparent position. Did that give time enough, Harry wondered, for what he had to do?

His small flotilla of power boats bobbed up and down

between the Penny Islands and Sexton in a channel almost a mile wide and at that point nearly two miles from the Coast Guard station. Harry's plan was to hug the Penny Islands on his starboard, move even farther away from the station, make a quick dash across the channel, and hide behind Sexton, waiting for another dark of the moon. Then he would lead his boats back through the narrow channel between Sexton and Captree islands, keeping a three-mile distance from the Coast Guard station, until he was safely in the inlet and racing for the open sea.

It had been a successful maneuver in the past, mainly because Harry had never attempted it except with heavy cloud cover or no moon at all. But the scud tonight was different, treacherously so. It could not be depended on for more than a few minutes at a time. Harry checked the moon's position again and made up his mind to take the maneuver piecemeal, step by step. If this brought him late to the rendezvous with the ship, so be it. He glanced at his watch. Eleven; sixty minutes to rendezvous.

Harry waved his fleet ahead, gunned his engines, and shot northward, in tight to the Penny Islands's shoreline, the *Deirdre* sending back immense sheets of salt spray that half blinded him. He knew the waters were extremely shoal at this point, but none of his fleet drew much more than a few inches, unloaded. Only the *Deirdre* drew more water than that, mainly because Harry had ballasted her with nearly a hundred small bags of beach sand to keep her silhouette low to the water.

Glancing back at the low-lying spread of Fire Island,

Harry watched the lighthouse's yellow ray sweep over-head. The Coast Guard station was almost invisible at this distance. He pulled the wheel hard port and sent the *Deirdre* slicing across the choppy water to the far side of Sexton Island. Then he pulled her into a slight cove and waited for the rest of his flotilla to make the run across open water. One by one, the boats pulled safely into shelter, bows high, wakes creamy. The last one had just streaked through when the scud opened up across the face of the moon.

"Goddamn, that was pretty, Harry."

Regan nodded. "Gorgeous good luck, Timmy."

He wiped the salt spray from his face and squinted down into the shallow cuddy cabin. Timmy was over sixty now, not terribly agile, but with enough muscle to make himself useful on these expeditions. He claimed a remote kinship with Harry on his mother's side, but this was not the reason Harry would allow only Timmy in the *Deirdre* on such nights. He had other men with clearer eyes and sharper ears who could handle a boat or a gun or a case of booze better than Timmy.

He'd met Timmy in a seedy side-street bar in Tampa some years back, while on a gun-buying mission. Timmy had been a supply sergeant in the A.E.F. He still had elderly buddies in the nearby arsenal depot who, over a few beers, had been willing to divert some equally elderly Springfields Harry's way at the ridiculous price of two dollars apiece. Timmy's price for serving as intermediary had been equally ridiculous: he wanted only to ship along on the gun-running mission.

The trip had been absolutely without incident the first few days. They'd headed south, the two of them, in a 27-foot ketch with a 20-horse auxiliary engine, every conceivable space below decks crammed with Springfields and ammo. After taking on fresh water they'd started the long reach across the Straits of Florida to a town called Cárdenas, some 75 miles east of Havana, where the Machado people were waiting with lovely leather bags of $5 gold pieces.

Somewhere along the way, one of those tricky autumn storms that spring up below the horse latitudes spun the ketch off course. They had been somewhere along the Tropic of Cancer, as near as Harry could figure it, between 22 and 24 degrees north. The storm demasted the ketch, ripped off the rudder, and left them. They drifted helplessly for two weeks, water and food completely gone, engine shot, their skin cracking from the intense sun, their lips caked with sores, throats parched, and worst of all, most of the Springfields jettisoned overboard to give them better flotation.

By the time they washed ashore at George Town, on Great Exuma, some 400 miles to the east, Timmy had sworn off adventure for what little remained of his life. But a year ago, when he'd gotten wind of Harry's new line of work, he'd trekked north to be with him again. Harry had long ago decided that Timmy was an excitement addict and suffered terribly when away from it too long.

Of all the motives a man might have, Harry had decided, this was probably least suspect. In the long run he would rather have a man who loved excitement for its own sake than one out strictly for money or revenge or, worst of all, a political man.

Staring now through the faintly moonlit night at his fleet of small craft, Harry wondered if any of them had been spotted by some sharp-eyed Coastguardsman with a good pair of night binoculars even though the moon had been obscured. The few minutes they were resting here, waiting for the scud to cover the moon again, would give Harry time to see what kind of reaction the station might have had to such a sighting.

He didn't know Lt. Ashley too well. The man hadn't been on the island that long, although Harry knew he was something of a native. The reports he had gotten of Ashley led him to believe the man was a by-the-numbers player. The two times he had run across Ashley face to face had been a little disturbing, though, as if the man weren't in complete control of himself.

"Were you with me the night Ashley's boat hailed us?" he asked Timmy.

"Ain't I always, Harry? It was late September last year, about a mile outside the inlet, and us heading straight out to sea after another pickup."

Harry smiled. "Did you get any sense of him being a gigantic brain, Timmy?"

"What's that?"

"You know, a genius at his work, a big-time thinker."

"Not that son-of-a-bitch Long Island clamfucker."

Harry shook his head. "Bad mistake to take a man the way he seems, Timmy."

"What other way have you got to take him?"

Harry shrugged. "What if I'd taken you at face value, Timmy? Just another rumdum A.E.F. scrounger, hanging around Florida waiting for your pension to come through?"

Timmy's face went blank for a moment. Then, in the moonlight, Harry could see his thin mouth split in a wide grin, revealing the two dark gaps in his front teeth. "What the hell else was I, Harry?" the older man asked.

Both men chuckled. Scud began to filter across the face of the moon now. Harry glanced at it very briefly. "Take awhile, yet."

He stared through the darker night at the Coast Guard station and could discern no unusual activity. It was possible that Ashley might be waiting to nail him as he rammed out of the inlet, full speed ahead, but it didn't seem likely.

Harry reviewed Ashley's legal alternatives, assuming one of his men had spotted the fleet of powerboats. First, of course, he could doubt the sighting, batten down the hatches, and go back to sleep. This Ashley would never do. His two brief encounters with the man had convinced Harry that Ashley was dedicated to his work. His alternative course would be to keep the fleet under surveillance while deciding what was to be done next. For example, Ashley could have the fleet shadowed through the night to its rendezvous with the freighter, swoop in, and battle it out with both the powerboats and the larger ship. That guaranteed a lot of action but, at night, damned few results. If Harry were in charge of the Coast Guard's

cutters and chasers he would send half of them to tail the
rum fleet and mobilize the other half just inside the inlet.
When the rum boats returned, laden with heavy cases of
booze, the two Coast Guard forces would catch them in
the narrow inlet, bottle them up and run them aground
or sink them at their leisure.

The latter, and better, plan, Harry realized with some
satisfaction, was only possible if Ashley were sure the
fleet would be returning along the route they had used
to go out to sea. But he had no such guarantee. The rum
boats could as easily run their cargo up on the beach at
intervals along the 40-mile surf and continue the operation by hand over the dunes and thickets.

"Ain't it about time to get moving, Harry?"

Harry glanced at the moon again and found it almost
lost in the scud. Only a faint oval patch of whitish cover
betrayed its place in the sky and the scud seemed to be
solid enough for several miles to windward. He sighed.

"S'matter, Harry?"

"Just thinking. It's no bed of roses being in Ashley's
shoes. And I'll be goddamned if it's any cinch being in
ours, either. I think of those Machado boys waiting on
the beach at Cárdenas for us with those little leather sacks
full of gold coin and I wonder why the hell I ever took
on this job."

"Shit, they ain't still waiting."

"No, but somebody else is, somewhere. The ABC boys
in Cuba are buying guns, I hear. Mario Menocal's group
is in the market. Machado's days are numbered down

there and, meanwhile, there's boodle to be made, Timmy."

"Guns is a lot of trouble, Harry." Timmy thought this over for a moment. "Heavy and awkward and not that many buyers. Booze is heavy, but, God, the buyers just flock to you."

Harry seemed not to have heard. "I was in Mexico with Obregon," he said, more to himself than the older man. "I was on the other side, buying the guns. That's how I realized the kind of money you could make in that line. This Calles, now, can't last. He's got the priests against him all over Mexico and that means he's got the women against him and that means he's got a good number of the softheaded men against him, to boot. That bunch of Cristeros down there, they'll be buying weapons damned soon, if they haven't stolen enough already."

"Don't seem right, you selling at a profit to a Catholic."

Harry laughed softly. "Every once in a while, I forget you're stupid, Timmy. The only reason I love you is you're stupid enough to throw in with me."

Timmy seemed offended. "Don't seem right, that's all. You and me being Catholics and them Cristeros being Catholics and fighting to keep this Calles from stealing all the church land."

Harry glanced at the moon again. He could find no trace of it beneath the heavy cloud cover. "I know a Marine master gunnery sergeant in Santo Domingo who can sell me Enfields in their original cases. Never been used. Never even been opened. He's got them hidden

93

away in a little shack near the Haitian border, down by the sea. Even his Captain doesn't know what happened to those Enfields. He'll sell them to me at $25 apiece and the Cristeros will pay me $50 apiece. It's a two-night sail across the Gulf to a landing point just above Veracruz. You game?"

Timmy moistened his lips. "How many rifles are there, Harry?"

"A gross."

"That's nearly four thousand bucks we make?"

"Check."

"When can we leave, Harry?"

Harry punched the older man lightly in the shoulder. "You're a gorgeous Catholic, Timmy. Selling rifles to Catholic rebels at better than a hundred percent profit?"

Timmy looked crestfallen. "You mean they ain't no Enfields? It was one of your jokes?"

"Oh, no. They're there. And the prices are right."

"So, then, why . . . ?"

Harry stood up in the *Deirdre* and made hand signals to the next boat behind him. He reached down and tickled the carburetors on the twin Fords. Then, taking the controls, he shoved the gas feeds forward. The *Deirdre* seemed to surge up out of the water as she lunged ahead.

One by one the rest of Harry's fleet churned up the shallow water as the boats sped out of shelter and, curving northwest around the farther side of Sexton Island, began the run south toward the inlet in the teeth of the wind. In the darkness, Harry knew, the only eyes in the whole flotilla belonged to him. The rest of his boats were following his wake, trusting that he could keep them out of shoal water and, at the same time, out of sight of the station.

Harry reflected now that this was something very much like the blind leading the blind. With the wind in his face he could only see a few yards ahead in this kind of darkness. Only his previous scouting of the area by day and by night had given him any trustworthy knowledge of the shorelines and depths.

Most of his people were amateurs in everything but clamming, Harry realized. Although they used boats ten months of the year and lived with water on both sides of them most of their lives, they rarely looked at a chart or knew how to read it. Nor was any of the information on the geodetic charts considered useful by them. When a man spends his day on Great South Bay raking in a few bushels of clams, running aground in shoal water means very little. He can simply wait a few hours for the tide to turn. In the slow-wheeling, inexorable rhythm of Fire Island life, a few hours out of a day, even a day completely wasted, meant nothing.

Harry completed the run between Sexton and Captree islands. With a long look at the seemingly quiet Coast Guard station, he headed the *Deirdre* hard starboard and gave his hand signal for full speed ahead.

They were in the inlet now and the tide was more or less neutral. There were times, Harry knew, when trying to buck the incoming tide in this narrow channel was more than even his overpowered craft could do. And there were a few well-remembered times when an outgoing tide and an offshore wind had forced a bay boat out into the Atlantic mists, never to be heard of again.

Harry reached forward and lifted out of the cuddy cabin a one-gallon tin of methyl alcohol. He sloshed it about for a moment, hefting its weight, and decided it wasn't full enough to waste any now on the *Deirdre*'s engines. No one was pursuing them, yet. Better to hoard the methyl till later.

"The wicked flee," Harry said aloud, almost involuntarily.

"What flea?"

"When none pursueth," Harry finished. He turned back to smile at Timmy and then decided against it. The old man might think it was some sort of reflection on him.

Harry watched the inlet widen on either side of him. To starboard, the low-lying hulk of Captree and Gilgo was a darker line on an almost invisible horizon. To port, suddenly, with an abruptness that always took his breath away, there was nothing, nothing at all except the limitless sweep of the chill, deep Atlantic.

Harry felt his jaw muscles tense. He cut the rudder hard port and sent the *Deirdre* straight ahead into the nothingness of ocean.

Chapter 12

". . . a blue room, a new room, for-two room, where we can . . ."

The wind-up Victrola slowed abruptly and, as the turntable stopped spinning, the tenor's words fell from baritone to bass to silence. Ellen Purvis gave a sharp sigh of exasperation, stopped the turntable, and cranked up the Victrola again. She let the cactus needle in the pickup arm ride in the same groove. When she released the control again, the acoustic speaker box squawked wildly and the tenor resumed his Pollyanna vision of bliss with snap and precision.

"We will thrive on, keep alive on, just nothing but kisses, with Mister and Missus on little blue chairs. We'll—"

Ellen slammed the pickup arm across the surface of the shellac record, silencing the tenor with a horrifying howl, as if he had been swallowed by a gigantic hound.

"Idiot!" Ellen screamed.

She flipped down the Victrola top and let it run itself down unseen. Then she strode as far as she could across the living room of the beach cottage. She glanced about her for a moment, not looking for anything in particular, but more as if measuring how much cubic air she had to exhaust before suffocating.

She badly missed a telephone. On the mainland of Long Island, her parents' home in Sayville had been one of the first with a phone, as far back as 1923, when Ellen was still in high school. As her friends' families got phones, Ellen got into the habit of keeping in touch with them that way. She had even formed the habit of calling shops that had telephones to give orders for deliveries. It had been a terrible extravagance, of course, but on a rainy day it certainly beat trying to walk to the shop.

When Jim Purvis had married her last year, Ellen had had no idea he planned to live all year round on Fire Island. It was something few sane people did, generally older folks who'd lived on the beach most of their lives. Even so, Ellen knew, when their children grew up, damned few had the stomach for the long, icy winters. It had been Jim's idea to set himself up in business as a contractor on Fire Island, building cottages he was certain many people would want in the years to come.

So far, after more than a year on this Godforsaken beach, the only money Jim had made was with Harry Regan. Fortunately, Jim's boat was powerful enough to interest Harry and, probably even more fortunately for

Jim, Ellen had also caught Harry's eye. Otherwise Jim would still owe money on both the house and the boat and would be even deeper in debt than before. As it was, thanks to Harry, he owned everything free and clear and had a few thousand in the bank, none of which Ellen could touch.

"Christ," she said aloud.

A phone wasn't that expensive, even here on the beach. The Coast Guard stations had been responsible for bringing over a telephone cable. Once that was laid, phone installation didn't cost a lot more than on the mainland. But Jim was too cheap for it. Or maybe just too mean.

That was probably it, Ellen reflected. He hated the idea of her keeping in touch with her friends and her family. That was it.

The only excitement up or down the whole beach was Harry Regan and him she had to share with every floozy he could find. On occasion one of the Coast Guard boys would stop by, ostensibly to get information on smuggling activity. They called when Jim was out in the bay, clamming.

Although she always took chances where Harry was concerned, she saw no reason to go completely crazy over any of the Coastguardsmen. One of them, a fellow her own age named Kinch who occasionally brought her little gifts, always took care to arrive alone. His gifts were fairly simple-minded—a box of chocolates one time and a fifth of Dewar's another (coals to Newcastle)—but there had been a day when Jim had been over on the mainland on business, with what amounted to a guarantee of being off the Beach at least eight hours. That had been Kinch's lucky day and, since then, Ellen had occasionally favored him when the coast seemed clear enough.

What the hell, she wondered, did Jim expect her to do with her days on this stretch of sand? Taking care of this shack he called a house used up very little time. Walking the beach alone had limited appeal for her. Listening to records had long ago palled. She had read all the books she could find. Jim refused to buy a radio. Gardening in the barren sand was out of the question, unless you simply planted more dune grass or poison ivy.

It wasn't as if she had turned into the town whore. There was only Harry and Kinch, and not even him too often. Oh, and another Coastguardsman named Spanier. And that one time when some dapper little man in a colorful bathing suit had wandered down from Ocean Beach, claiming to be a close friend of Flo Ziegfeld. And one of the maintenance men in Point O' Woods. Money didn't enter into it, so it wasn't whoring. She knew what it was, but it wasn't whoring.

Ellen sighed again, that short burst of pent-up breath, and began to pace the living room. The night wind had died momentarily, leaving a total silence that frightened her more than sounds did. By a trick of placement, the ridge of the dune cut off the sound of the ocean's surf except when the wind was just right. Now, with Jim away for most of the night and Harry with him, there was no sound and no hope of a sound.

It was the same as any other night, God knew, but it

was worse because there was no hope of human companionship. Even Jim was better than nothing, although not much.

Harry was the best, of course. There was no one like him. Ellen had met a man like Harry only once before in her life. She'd been a little girl, perhaps six years old, when an A.E.F. buddy of her father had dropped in for a visit. She hadn't known till later that he'd come to borrow money. At the time, she'd listened to his wild stories and believed all of them. He'd rustled rubies in Brazil and slave girls in Macao. He'd fought with Pancho Villa. He'd fought with the Kuomintang against Chinese warlords and with the warlords against the Kuomintang. He'd stolen pearls from headhunters in the Solomon Islands. He'd fought the Rif in the Sahara. He'd fought with Kornilov against the Bolsheviki and had been a colonel in Wrangel's White Army. And now he had a plan for stealing a silver mine in Bolivia and all he needed was a thousand U.S. dollars. In a year, his backers would get back ten for every dollar they invested and he guaranteed that—

Ellen stopped and stared out the window. The ragged scud parted for a moment to let the moon shine through. A minute later the clouds closed over the moon again and the night was as dark as it was silent.

She wondered what made men like Harry Regan so attractive. Was it because they seemed to be the only ones left with a little life in them? The only ones to move out and do and dare and have a laugh doing it?

The one year she had been at junior college they had

made her read books none of her friends had ever heard of, by people with names like Fielding and Defoe and Smollet, Englishmen who wrote about whores and rascals and adventurers as if they were not only the equal of ordinary people but in some way greatly superior to most.

It had puzzled Ellen and when she'd asked her professor about it, he'd been no help. There had been no one she could ask. No one had read any of these books, although they were supposed to be very well-known. But this one night last December Jim had gone to the mainland for kerosene oil and Harry had dropped by for a few hours in bed with her.

"Nothing gets done by routine people," Harry had said, "except routine stuff. I don't knock routine stuff. Somebody has to do it. But it isn't exactly what moves the world ahead, is it, darlin'?"

"But why write books about criminals and such? Famous books, too."

"It depends on what's a criminal," Harry had replied.

"A man who kills another man is a criminal."

"Yes."

"But if he's a doughboy in the Argonne and the fellow he kills is a Heinie, then he isn't a criminal."

"That's different."

"No. That's exactly the same. Murder is murder. Only one thing makes a difference, what name the government gives it."

"You're saying that to excuse your own life, Harry."

"I'm saying it because it's true. Governments tell you what's a crime and what isn't, when you can kill and loot and burn, and when you can't."

He had rolled over restlessly on the bed and sat up, feeling for cigarettes in the pocket of the shirt hung on the chair. "I've made my living both ways, inside and outside the law. Mostly I've made it on the edge between. Your routine kind of person doesn't see that the edge is man-made. He's invented a story that God made right and wrong, not governments. It's comforting to him. Your routine kind of man doesn't want to make decisions for himself. He's happier if he believes they've already been made. And he's as happy as a pig in shit if he actually believes the decision's been made by God."

"That's Jim," she had murmured, "a pig in shit."

"Don't make that mistake. He's not a routine kind of man."

"The hell he isn't."

Harry had found a cigarette and lighted it, giving it to her for a drag. "Jim is going through something temporary. Some day he'll come out the other side, lay open your back with a blacksnake whip, and leave you to bleed to death here on the beach while he goes off to find excitement. What he'll find is the sheriff waiting across the bay to arrest him. Jim isn't routine. He's just unlucky."

"Do you think he'd really . . . ?"

"Guaranteed, darlin'. He knows about you and me and you and the entire Coast Guard detachment and one of these days when the thought of it has got him so riled he can't get it up any more with you, he'll try murder. If I were a lawyer fellow, I'd do a study of the number of women murdered by men who couldn't get it up for them."

Ellen had snuggled in against him. "A murder you'll never commit."

Harry laughed softly. "That's because you don't use the same hold on me that you use on Jim."

Ellen was afraid to pursue that line for fear she would be treated to too much of Harry's rather bleak view of her. He had a habit of almost casually stripping her of all defenses. To distract him now, she switched the subject around.

"You don't give human beings much credit, do you, Harry? I mean, such a crazy reason for committing murder. Like an animal."

Harry shook his head. "I bow to your superior wisdom, darlin'. I love the way you people pick out the most human thing—something no animal's ever been known to do—and call it inhuman or bestial or something as silly."

"You people? What are you, Harry, the man from Mars?"

"If I were, darlin', I'd have ticked off the human animal long ago."

"Such as?"

Harry shrugged. "First off, a carnivorous predator of extreme cunning and great dexterity. And then, perhaps, I'd say he's the only animal who regularly, consistently murders his own species and fails to eat the flesh. No other animal kills regularly unless it's hungry. And only man has managed to bamboozle himself into thinking he's something special. He's invented a whole fairy story to excuse his close similarity to other animals and to make him seem something far apart from them. And that gives him another reason for murder . . . he'll kill people who don't believe the fairy story."

"God's a fairy story?"

"Along with your immortal soul and mine. Let me tell you about men, darlin', as the madam says to the new girl from the boondocks. A man's dirtier than a pig, more bloodthirsty than a tiger, more treacherous than a tarantula, less friendly than a diamondback rattler, and less particular than a hyena. They'll do any dirty thing they have a mind to, no matter who it hurts, and find a dozen brave excuses for it, making themselves out heroes and saints. Man is the only animal that talks, and the only one that tells lies."

"I think I'm hearing one right now."

Ellen sighed and wriggled closer to Harry, trying to interest him in her body again. "It's a good thing you don't hate women the way you hate men."

Harry laughed. "Man, darlin', not men. I include both sexes, although I've found women generally more decent than men."

"What woman wouldn't be decent to you, Harry, if you gave her half a chance?"

His eyes hooded slightly under their sandy red brows, the pale lashes half covering Harry's bright green irises.

He drew heavily on the cigarette and sent a thin plume of smoke into the air. Then he turned away from Ellen to stub out the cigarette. "Time to be off. Jim's on his way back for sure."

"So quickly? We've got at least another hour."

"I've got things to do."

"And other women to lay."

He swung his legs over the edge of the bed and stared at the layer of fine, shiny reddish-blonde hairs on his thighs and calves.

"Harry?"

"What?"

He had nothing further to say to her, and she knew it, but she desperately wanted him to stay, even a few more minutes. "Tell me something, Harry."

"Anything, love."

"If you feel that way about people, shouldn't you just shoot yourself or something?"

"Or run amok and kill as many as I can before they get me," he suggested.

"Yes. Or something. But, instead . . ." She paused for a moment, suddenly shy. "I hear stories about . . . I mean, they say you . . . you're not just in this for money."

"Do they."

"They say you've got other reasons. That the money doesn't all go into your pocket. That it's for something else, something big overseas."

"Is that what they say?" Harry had pulled on his long-johns and was now wriggling into his jeans.

"They say you're a Bolshevik or something. The money's going to Russia. Or it's going to Cuba. Or Ireland."

"Or the moon." Harry stood up and began tucking in his shirt. He turned to grin at Ellen and the bright flash of teeth seemed to catch at a corner of her heart and give it a queer turn.

Now, remembering that time in December, she wondered whether Harry would ever give any more of himself to her than to anyone else, to that Maeve Curran bitch who was playing house with him, for instance, or to some of the show business floozies who summered in Ocean Beach and kept Harry hopping during the short nights.

She decided that if she felt about humans the way Harry did, there wouldn't be one of them to whom she could confide anything more personal than the time of day.

And yet, if he did feel that way, why were there all the rumors linking him with do-good plots and harebrained political schemes? If he hated people, he would be out to do them in for his own good, wouldn't he?

Ellen paced nervously across the living room and flipped up the top of the Victrola. A man like Harry attracted crazy rumors. One of the Coastguardsmen had sworn to Ellen that Harry Regan had been in on the kidnaping of Aimee Semple McPherson last year and had later fixed the Dempsey-Tunney fight to let Gene win. Her own father, her own fatheaded, fat-assed father across the bay in Sayville, had warned her once about associating with that Regan fellow. He vaguely remembered him being connected with the Sacco and Vanzetti scandal.

She lifted off the record and placed a new one on the turntable, switched off the machine, and wound it up tightly. Then she examined the cactus needle and found that she had snapped off the fine point when she'd slammed down the tone arm before. Removing the needle, she squinted slightly as she put it into the little device that rubbed a sandpaper wheel against it and gave it a new point.

Then she replaced the needle and started the Victrola. The saxophones mewed creamily. "In a little Spanish town," the soprano sang, enunciating each word with earache clarity, "'twas on a night like this. Stars were . . ."

No, they weren't, Ellen thought. There are no nights like this anywhere else.

Chapter 13

Maxie's East Moriches place was a rather large three-story house just off the Montauk Road and a few yards from Seatuck Cove. He had chosen it carefully to give him mobility by land and water. The old house's stables could hold four trucks and two cars if necessary, while the private boat landing on the cove had a covered boat-house that could conceal two cruisers, a 26-footer and a 32-footer with Liberty aircraft engines.

The house had originally belonged to an elderly retired optometrist and his wife who had moved there from Manhattan. Maxie had made them an offer for the house that could not be ignored, double what they'd paid for it. There had been some delay on their part in making a decision, due mainly to the optometrist's wife's reluctance to uproot and resettle herself this late in life. They had gone back to Manhattan one afternoon to attend a funeral and had never been seen again. Maxie's bill of sale had two signatures on it, witnessed the day of the old couple's departure.

Despite the pains he had taken to secure the place, however, Maxie used it as more of a rendezvous than a headquarters. Heinckel's people, or any other night-laborers he could scrub up from the surrounding area, knew the Moriches place well and this made it unsafe as a headquarters. But it was ideal as a rallying point. From there, often blindfolded, the volunteer labor could be trucked over the Montauk Road to Quogue or Hampton Bays. Or they might be taken by cruiser through Moriches Bay, past Westhampton Beach to a point on Tiana Beach near the Shinnecock Inlet.

It was there, on an absolutely deserted slope of sea-grass behind a high dune fronting on the Atlantic, that Maxie moored the converted 50-foot corvette he had bought as surplus from the Canadian Navy in 1925. Its flush decks made it hard to spot in any halfway heavy sea. It was faster than any rum freighter, or any of Regan's motley armada, and it could run rings around the Coast Guard picket boats.

It had cost Maxie—or rather Maxie's principals—more than $50,000, unarmed. Maxie had been somewhat conservative in the rearmament of the corvette. He had given it twin 50-caliber water-cooled machine guns bow and stern and two more on the bridge amidships.

He had toyed for a while with the idea of restoring to the corvette its original 100 mm. gun emplacements, two of them, capable of handling armor-piercing shells. But some of his principals' advisers had explained to Maxie that the kind of adversaries he would be going up against were carrying little more than boiler-plate. Maxie himself knew that in a running fight victory went to the side that could throw the most slugs, whatever their caliber, not to the side that managed to lob a few big ones over.

His principals had supplied Harry with a captain after their own heart, if not his, a dour, nasty-voiced Frenchman named Lacoste, after the tennis player who had won the singles championship last year. Maxie assumed his real name would be something else. As long as he kept quiet and took orders he could be Clemenceau himself, for all Maxie cared.

Heinckel's men had collected at eleven o'clock at the Moriches place. They were being ferried out to the Hamptons now in the Packard touring car and a Duesenberg phaeton belonging to one of Maxie's principals, four men in one, six in the other. With the crew he had standing by, Maxie would have twenty-one people to man the corvette. Between them, if everybody did his job right, Maxie would nip Harry Regan the way a squirrel nips a nut and cracks it wide open. But they had to get going soon.

Maxie stood in the wheelhouse of the corvette next to Lacoste. The ship's diesels vibrated heavily beneath Maxie's feet. The thin soles of his pointed, elegant shoes transmitted the vibration with a buzzing intensity that made the bottoms of Maxie's feet tingle and sweat. A thin stink of diesel fuel hung in the damp sea air like a wisp

111

of brownish fog. Maxie hated the smell. The Duesenberg arrived, headlights darkened.

"We better get moving, Frenchy."

Lacoste's unshaven face wrinkled like a monkey's as he turned to squint at Maxie. "Now?"

Maxie jerked his thumb toward the southeast, where the Shinnecock Inlet lay in darkness and wind. Heinckel's men were filing aboard. "Let's vamoose."

Lacoste muttered something obscene to himself. Then he raised his voice and shouted "Cast off stern lines!"

Chapter 14

Lt. Ashley blinked away the faint haze that seemed to obscure his vision. He refocused the 7 x 50 night glasses, zeroing in on whatever it was he thought he had seen moving seaward through the inlet.

"Chief," he called.

He was standing in a little attic room at the very top of the Coast Guard station, hardly more than a lookout cubbyhole. The low-lying cover over the moon came and went with such infuriating trickiness that he could never be quite certain of what he had seen. If he'd seen anything at all.

Below him he could hear Heydt's deliberate steps, not slow, for that would be obvious insubordination, but not fast enough either, damn him.

"Sir."

Ashley turned on Chief Heydt and watched his emotionless face for a long moment. Then he passed the night glasses to him. "See what you can make out in the inlet."

Heydt studied the blackness for a long moment, sweeping the glasses in sideways, overlapping arcs. Then he handed them back to Ashley. "Nothing, sir." His jaw clamped tight shut.

"I thought I—" Ashley stopped himself. He knew very well the kind of tricks his eyes played during the night watch. The Coast Guard had taught him never to trust the faint movements he might discern in blackness without the confirmation of another pair of eyes.

The retinas sometimes produced faint images all on their own as a result of nervous tension or lack of sleep or a dozen other factors. Of course, Ashley reminded himself bitterly, the Coast Guard didn't even begin to list what might happen to a man's vision if he'd already consumed at least a pint of whisky within the past hour.

"That will be all, Chief," he snapped. The mint he was chewing seemed to perfume the air.

Heydt started back down the stairs, obviously glad to be leaving. It bothered Ashley that he had let the bastard off that easily. What bothered him even more was that he was sure Heydt knew something about tonight, something more than he had reported. They all did, even stupid little Ensign Jorgensen. They were probably all in the pay of Harry Regan.

"Just a second," he called to Heydt.

By the waiting stiffness of his back, by its insolent arch, the Chief showed his disdain, or so it seemed to Ashley.

"I don't like what's going on tonight," he told Heydt. The other man turned to watch him with mild, expressionless eyes.

"Something's up. You know it. I know it. But we're not going to sit around here on our asses and let it happen."

Ashley watched the effect of this on the Chief. Heydt's eyes failed to widen, shift, or narrow. They continued to regard Ashley with total disinterest or, rather, with the kind of attention one gives a child who has been prattling nonsense for far too long.

"What do you suggest, Chief?"

Heydt's eyes narrowed very slightly then. "Suggest for what, sir?"

"To head off what's happening."

"I'm not sure I know what the Captain means, sir."

"The Captain means a shipment's being landed tonight, and you know it damned well, too."

Heydt's eyes went blank again. "If that's the case, sir, I suppose the best suggestion would be to send out a patrol to intercept. If you'll give me some idea of the rendezvous, we can—"

"If I knew that," Ashley cut in savagely, "this whole, idiotic . . ."

He tried to master his temper. The colitis pain had started up inside him again, despite the whisky and aspirin. He was usually in much better control of himself. The combination of being drunk, of being in agony, and of being baited by Heydt in that flat-faced deadpan way of his was what had softened him and he knew it.

"About face on the double," Ashley ordered. He followed Heydt, the two of them jogging down the spiral stairs to the radio room. "Assemble the men."

The entire company, with the exception of ten on leave or liberty, gathered in the next few minutes. Jorgensen, eyes tiny with sleep, arrived still tying his tie.

"Call the roll," Ashley ordered.

Heydt's orderly called the roll and reported a total complement on hand of thirty men. Ashley took a step toward the formation in which the men stood at attention.

"Out there tonight," he began, "somewhere along the twelve-mile line, there's a freighter hove to and waiting. The patrol raised her twice tonight.

"It's not the best wind and sea to try landing a shipment, but for all we know these rumrunners may be in a desperate situation. There may be good reasons why they'll try a landing. When that happens, we intend to be on the spot."

Ashley stopped and waited. Being at attention, none of the men spoke. But Ensign Jorgensen looked as if he would have liked to say something. Before he could, Ashley continued addressing the men.

"I'm the first one to recognize that this may be a wild goose chase. Ensign Jorgensen's patrol earlier may have scared off the criminals. They may have decided to land at some other point, even some other shore. It's little enough chance we take, trying to intercept them. But if we stay here, we certainly won't find anything."

He paused for a second and then jabbed a finger in

Jorgensen's direction. The boy's normally rosy cheeks went crimson. "You're in command of the lead vessel," he said. "You take the cutter to the spot where you first raised the freighter."

Ashley turned to Heydt. "You'll remain here with the radio men," he ordered. "I'll take the launch." He called six men by name, motioning them out of formation to stand by him.

"I've got the six best marksmen in the company," he said. "We'll use rifles. The cutter crew has the heavier weapons and grenade launchers and all the rest."

He waited again, but no one spoke and Jorgensen seemed to have lost any desire to. "I don't normally like to take a twenty-eight-foot launch into the Atlantic at night in a strong sea, but none of our other craft is fast enough for the assignment. And we need at least two vessels. Are there any questions?"

"Sir."

Ashley turned to face Heydt. If he could have found a reason, he would gladly have put a 30-30 slug between the man's flat, pale eyes. "Yes, Chief."

"With the Captain's permission, sir, what plan does the Captain have if the bootleggers try landing the shipment along the beach?"

"Your suggestion, Chief."

Heydt's face seemed to hide some suppressed emotion. "It might be good to detail a few men to patrol the shore on foot and by beach buggy."

"And if they encounter any smugglers?"

Heydt shrugged. "Well, sir, their presence might serve as a deterrent."

"I don't mind taking risks and I expect my men to take them. But two men in a beach buggy can do nothing against a force of rumrunners except turn tail or die."

"Just a suggestion, sir."

"A bad one." Ashley turned back to the men, a slight curve of triumph on his lips. He had clearly bested Heydt. He felt ready to best any of them.

"With the Captain's permission," Ensign Jorgensen said then, "I'll have an acetylene searchlight mounted on the launch. Otherwise you'll be in darkness."

Ashley nodded. "Good. We sail in five minutes. Dismissed." The formation broke up. "Let's get moving, men."

He watched them scatter to their various tasks. The pain in his gut was almost gone now. He turned to the radio men at their receiver panels. "Anything?"

Spanier shook his head. "Half hour to midnight, sir. Lindbergh's hit the point of no return."

Chapter 15

Shifting quarter restlessly, the wind seemed to be searching for something. It had veered a few points more to the east and now the long, copper-wire antenna on Harry Regan's shack began to cut into the wind with the low sound of sorrow and mourning.

Maeve woke up at once. She had never been a heavy sleeper, even as a child. The long, cold nights of Fire Island had always been filled with winds that spoke to her.

Winds moaned in grasses, hissed over sands. The low-lying prickle of a holly bush could rip ecstasies of unhappiness from the heart of the wind. Maeve would hear and respond. The wind's call reached her now.

She lay on her back, eyes open and staring at the low ceiling beams of the flimsy shack. Being alone in bed helped keep her awake. There had been very few nights in the past year when Harry hadn't been in this bed with her, eventually.

Not matter what woman he'd been with, he always came back to sleep. Maeve supposed a woman of any pride would have put a stop to all this long ago. She felt sure most of the Islanders pitied her. From the furious curses her own mother leveled at her, she knew they considered Maeve a whore and a fool to keep house for the likes of Harry Regan.

He would never marry. He was permanently unfaithful. And some fine night he would be shot to death. Where would Maeve be then, soiled beyond redemption?

She had no idea where she'd be then. Her soul, of course, was doomed utterly. For her sins, unconfessed this whole long year—never to mass or confession or communion—she was certain that when death released it, her soul would flap its black, sodden way to hell.

Maeve shifted uneasily in the cold bed. She required Regan's body next to her. She required his cool voice telling her there was no hell, no soul. She knew all of it to be lies, but she required his body and his voice.

The nights when he was out bringing in the shipments were no good for her. She slept badly then. The wind would wake her and whisper horrible thoughts in her head. For all his bones stuck through his skinny flesh, for all his blasphemies and cheating, Regan was a warm comfort to her. She supposed that if ever she could talk about all of it to a priest, she would quickly learn that Regan was a judgment on her, a thorn in her heart and God's own special version of hell on earth. Not that she could ever talk about it. She smiled at the thought of telling a priest.

Maeve had never slept with any man before Regan. She was twenty and she knew now she was forever tied to Regan. He had taken everything, her maidenhead, her soul, her good name, her mind, and her heart. All of these she had held out to him and he had taken as offhandedly as if she had handed him a ham sandwich.

Maeve rolled on her side and stared out the window, trying to see the night wind. None of that meant much to Regan, she supposed. He'd taken as much, as a matter of course, from so many other women. It was easy to see herself as nothing more than just another home convenience for Harry.

In the dark, Maeve knew, any other of his women could perform as satisfactorily and he'd never recognize the difference. In the dark, she told herself, we are all the same, men and women.

But in the light, Regan is going to know who the bloody hell he's dealing with. He's going to learn, she thought, that I am the one he will marry and leave off smuggling for and have kids with.

Me. None of the others. For them he had nothing but that hot, smoking cock of his. There was never anything more between him and them because nobody wanted any more. But Maeve wanted as much more as there was. As much as he had taken from her, that much she wanted of him, his cynical soul wrapped in her body and forever in bondage to her. She wanted him enough to kill him.

Maeve grinned in the darkness at the fierceness of her

thought. Regan couldn't be killed. The pair of them would live forever. To the end of time he'd cheat on her and she'd require him beside her all the long, cold nights of eternity.

It might frighten another woman, she thought. Me it amuses. Maeve felt impatient, lying there, for the day when she could get Regan off the island for good. That way, she knew, he would really live forever and she with him.

She sighed, not with content or impatience, but in sorrow. She knew she would never leave this cursed island, nor would Regan. She had a sudden picture of him, like one of the High Kings of the Old Land, his bier piled high with green offerings as the funeral barge floated off, out into the mists of the sea, with the harpers' music in his ears. She saw herself beside him, the two of them floating off into the final mists of death.

Moaning more loudly now, the wind agreed.

The frontiersman is gone. So is the wilderness in which he roamed like any other animal, enjoying life in his own often peculiar way. Did the frontier breed eccentrics? Or were eccentrics the only men who could tame the frontier? No matter. The taming is over. We have no more room for eccentrics. In a single act, Lindbergh has shown us that only in the eccentric is there hope for the race. But his flight has shrunk our earth to a tiny ball, overcrowded, teeming with mediocrity. I hail this act as I must hail the bold and free in any form. But in my heart I mourn. His act is a last act. Albeit slowly, the curtain is descending on the human comedy.

Knut Hammarlund
(as quoted in *Smart Set,*
June, 1927)

Chapter 16

The May wind quickened, whipping spray off the wave-lets. Harry ducked below for a moment to wipe his face with a bit of towel. Timmy was huddled in the forward end of the cuddy cabin oiling a Thompson submachine gun by the faint light of the tiny kerosene lantern there. Harry had placed the lantern deep inside the cuddy where it could be seen by no one except the boat immediately behind him. Each boat in his flotilla used the same method of orienting the craft behind it so that all of them stayed in a relatively straight line as they made their way without running lights through the darkness.

They were bearing almost due east and had already passed the ocean side of the Coast Guard station at a distance from it of over three miles. This course would take them further away from the coast of Fire Island the more east they moved, since the shore itself ran slightly northeast.

Harry knelt beside Timmy and checked his compass bearing by the light of the lantern. The *Deirdre* heaved bravely and sank with slow dignity beneath them. Ballasted as she was, there was no unseemly bucking and heaving for the *Deirdre* until the sea got a good deal higher than this one.

Harry took the opportunity to recheck his "snail" magazines for the Luger Parabellum. He inserted the keylike tightening tool in the mechanism of each and gave it a slight twist. By the light of the lantern he could read the legend on one of the magazines: "Deutsche Waffen und Munitionsfabriken Berlin."

"*Achtung, kamerad,*" he told Timmy.

"Gotcha, Harry." Timmy winked.

Harry felt particularly exhilarated as he made his way back to the stern and unshipped the holder loops that kept the *Deirdre*'s tiller steady. He squinted into the rising spray. She'd been a sad old girl, the original Deirdre. Funny he should think of her right now and in this place. Perhaps it had been singing those songs at Goldie's house. Goldie was no sad old girl, she wasn't.

"Deirdre," Harry murmured aloud into the sharp May wind. "Deirdre of the Sorrows, wife of Conchobar, the filthy pig-king of Ulster."

"What's that, Harry?"

Harry nodded to Timmy. "I'm in mind of an old story, is all. Deirdre of the Sorrows." Harry settled himself more comfortably by the tiller. "She loved another. Naoise, son of Usnach, was his name and she fled with him to Scotland. But her husband lured Naoise back and killed him."

"Serves him right."

"And Deirdre died on Naoise's grave of a broken heart."

"Serves them both right."

"I had no idea you were such a moral man, Timothy."

"Me moral?" Timmy lifted the Thompson and gestured as if firing a burst across Harry's midriff, cutting him in two.

"Don't play games with that!"

"It ain't loaded, Harry." Timmy held up the drum magazine. "See?"

Harry nodded. "I figure Deirdre's husband was a bastard. He was king of Ulster, Timmy, and damned if ever I saw an Ulsterman who wasn't a shameful, lying, son-of-a-bitch murderer. Ain't it the truth?"

"God's truth."

"What if I told you I was an Ulsterman, Timmy?"

"But you ain't."

"How can you be sure? How do you know I'm really with the Organization." He gave the word its full Fenian pronunciation, "Organ-eye-zation."

"But you are."

"Maybe I lied. Maybe I'm just a common bootlegger. Maybe the money from this work doesn't get funneled back to the I.R.A."

"But it does."

"No one here can love or understand me," Harry sang

127

softly. He was feeling a bit giddy and knew it. "Oh, what hard-luck stories they all hand me." He continued the song, whistling.

"Harry."

"What."

"What call have you to spook up an old man with such lies?"

"How can I stop lying to you? You're a mean old fart and you keep asking for it." Harry checked the compass heading and glanced at his watch. Almost midnight. He headed the *Deirdre* very slightly to port and took an ENE bearing that kept him parallel with the Fire Island coast. He stared aft to make sure the boat behind him followed the change without mistake.

He had from time to time tried to see what, if anything, he could make out of the trailing boat. Occasionally he had caught a glimpse of what he took to be its skipper, Jim Purvis, by the very faint light of his own concealed lantern. But his reflected-light image was too thin to be trustworthy. The fact that he failed to see it now didn't unduly alarm Harry. He would see Jim in a few minutes or he wouldn't. Either way, he wouldn't really be certain the flotilla was firmly behind him until they actually closed with the freighter to begin unloading operations.

This was the part about leadership Harry Regan liked least, the fact that when you marched out front you were never quite sure who was following you, if anyone.

He was pretty sure Jim Purvis would keep him in sight.

Of all the men he recruited for these forays, Jim had the best sense of seamanship, which wasn't saying too much. But he also was motivated by the strongest greed. Harry supposed that if you were married to a dissatisfied bitch like Ellen, you had a pressing need for a lot of money, if not to gratify her, then to gratify yourself away from her.

He touched his earlobe, where Ellen had bitten him earlier tonight. A mean streak in her, no doubt of it. What she was doing to her husband . . .

Harry stared ahead, wanting to spot the freighter as soon as possible. Funny about motivation, he thought. Purvis wants money. Timmy wants excitement. The I.R.A. wants guns.

The Organization's plan had a lot to recommend it. The booze had originally been stolen in Scotland in the course of several raids on distilleries. The freighter was an old scow saved from scrapping. The crew were volunteers. It cost the I.R.A. a few tons of coal to get a thousand cases of Haig and Dewar's across the briny to Harry Regan.

Harry's own operation was pared to the bone as far as expenses went. Each man in the flotilla got a case for his night's pay. Boat owners got extra cases in lieu of rental fees. Purvis got a few more than the rest. When the Organization's trucks arrived in Islip later tonight, they would pick up, allowing for payoffs, breakage, and loss at sea, easily 900 cases of genuine Scotch whisky, worth more than a buck a bottle on the wholesale market, say twelve thousand simoleons for a night's work, more on the cases sold at retail.

That money was converted more or less on the spot to guns, ammo, and grenades which the same freighter loaded two days hence at a pier in Weehawken. She usually made the trip back to Ireland inside of two weeks. From start to finish—the raid on the distilleries to the delivery of munitions back in Ireland—it took the I.R.A. one month and a few dozen pounds of expenses to arm hundreds of men.

And this would be the eighth shipment Harry Regan had handled for the Organization in the past year. No knowing how many Irish volunteers had been armed so far this way. Thousands?

Harry stood up tall in the stern of the *Deirdre*. "There she is, half starboard."

Timmy scrambled out of the cuddy. "Christ, Harry, you done it beautiful."

The two men stood there watching the high hulk of the freighter turning slightly in the distance. Apparently, no one aboard the ship had seen them yet. In this kind of darkness, with the intermittent light of the moon, Harry decided, it would be a few more minutes before the low-lying *Deirdre* closed enough with the freighter to be seen.

Harry cut the engines to an idle and declutched, letting the driveshaft spin itself to a standstill. The forward movement of the *Deirdre* stopped almost abruptly and her bow settled down farther into the waves.

Harry stared astern, waiting for Purvis's boat to come into view. He wanted to be sure all his people were lined up and ready before he closed with the freighter and began the tricky business of unloading on the high seas.

Chapter 17

Farther east, the corvette knifed through the gathering waves at twenty knots an hour on its southwest run toward the delivery rendezvous.

One of the refinements Maxie had caused to be fitted into the ship was the installation of the radio room and its operator in the wheelhouse so that there need be no wasted time relaying messages from Sparks to Captain. Maxie stood next to Captain Lacoste, peering out at the darkness as the Frenchman adjusted the wheel from time to time. Behind him, Maxie could hear the faint bzzp-bzzp of a low-frequency Morse transmission.

"He's reporting," the radioman said. "I found him on another wavelength."

Maxie turned around. "Whuz the report?"

The radioman listened for a moment, scribbling on a pad of paper. "They rendezvous off Cherry Grove at the twelve-mile limit."

"Ast him is he sure." Maxie's tight little growl was another version, lower in pitch, of the Morse buzz. He watched the radioman spin off a great mass of clicks with his telegraph key. After a moment the low bzzp-bzzp resumed.

"Sure as he ever is," the radioman said at length.

"Now tell him to take care of the escape routes."

"Right, Maxie." The radioman loosed a flood of clicks. This time there was almost no wait for the bzzp-bzzp of the return message. "Says he's on his way. Signed off."

Maxie nodded and turned back to stare at the night. "You heard, Frenchie?"

"I hear. The name is Lacoste."

"Right, Frenchie."

"On zis ship, I am Captain Lacoste. Or get yourself another captain."

Maxie darted a sideways glance at Lacoste's wrinkled, unshaven face. The word he'd gotten—and passed on to his principals in Brooklyn—was that Regan would try to bring in a big shipment tonight, anything up to a thousand cases or more. Once he'd reported it to headquarters, Maxie was on the hook and had to deliver, if not the whole shipment, then enough of it to prove he could tackle Regan and win.

He couldn't afford to have one lousy Frog pilot screw up the works. "Right, Cap'n," he said ingratiatingly.

Lacoste's stubbly face flattened slightly as he grinned. He looked more like an ape than ever to Maxie. "We get along okay," he said, turning to bestow his simian grin on Maxie.

Lacoste's breath mingled good cognac with garlic in about equal proportions. It was, Maxie thought, like swimming in hot *tsimmes*, the concoction his mother made for him down on Hester Street. Only his mother took it easier on the garlic.

"How'd you like this job regular?" Maxie asked, simply to make conversation with a man whom after tonight he might never see again alive.

"Not bad pay. And the cognac is *le vrai Hennesey.*"

"Everything we handle is high-class merchandise, kiddo," Maxie assured him. "This ain't no schlach operation. Our connections go right to the top."

"That I know. What I don't know," Lacoste went on, "is why you do zis hijack thing. You also cook whisky too, no?"

"I'll tell the cockeyed world." Maxie stood there for a moment, wondering how a man like Lacoste could have been in and around the alky business without knowing the simple facts of life. Maybe he'd just come over from France. Otherwise, who didn't know?

Maxie peered out into the night. The wind slapped white foam off the tops of each wave like a bartender stropping the head off a schooner of beer.

"I'll tell you all about it some time, Fre—Cap'n Lacoste. Not tonight, though. I gotta million things to think about."

Which was a lie. On these runs, Maxie knew, there were always the long waits, the endless stretches of open sea before you came in hard and hit fast. A little action and it was over. Of course, he had never tackled Regan on anything this big before. He'd hijacked a dozen shipments of other leggers, all of them big, but Regan's full outfit he had yet to tangle with.

The word was they weren't connected with any of the Mick mobs in town. And they weren't unloading through any Wop or Mocky bunches. Maxie knew them all. The bunch he worked for had recently hooked up with a few more and some of the newspapers were starting to take notice. Murder, Incorporated, one of the blats put it. Stupid bastards.

Nobody understood the operation any better than this frog-brained whore-lapper Frenchman here. They all thought it had to do with killing people. Or cooking alky. Nobody'd ever put it all together the way it really was.

Maxie opened a fresh pack of Sweet Caporals, offered them to Lacoste and the radioman, then lighted the cigarettes for them. He blew out the flame and lighted his own with a fresh match. Maxie winked at Lacoste over the faintly Turkish-smelling smoke. "Bad luck for your poi-loos, too, huh?"

"Three on a match. *Très mal.*" Lacoste gave his monkey wink.

Maxie watched the blackness past the bow. He'd been a kid right out of uniform when the whole thing had started over here. Armistice had come before Maxie ever left training camp. So, when the Volstead Act became law, he was barely 21. Of course, Maxie recalled, he'd already built up some good Brooklyn connections, useful ones that led to jobs working the protection dodge on fruit sellers and dry cleaners and the rest of that scum.

Connected as he was, it wasn't too hard for Maxie to know what the Volstead Act really did. Everybody knew it outlawed making it and transporting it and selling it. But it didn't tell the big distillers what to do with their inventories of it.

And inventories was what the whole thing was all about. You let the stuff age. At any one time and place, you might have a million simoleons stashed away in oak barrels. That was a lot of kelp to take out of circulation. Along comes the government and tells you, forget it. Eat it. Stick it up your ass. But don't transport or sell it.

Maxie figured there had to be at least a billion smackers in inventory among all the distillers. They weren't going to just lie down, cut their throats, and die, for Christ's sake, no matter what the government told them. So they turned to people like Maxie's connections to get the stuff into circulation.

What else was there for the distillers? Go that road, or take bankruptcy. But mobs like Maxie's had to get themselves organized properly. It wouldn't do any more to have all the street fighting and machine gun ambushes and pineapple bombings. To handle a coast-to-coast job like that, the mobs had to pull together and organize coast-to-coast. And, pretty soon . . .

"Why you no answer me?" Lacoste asked.

Maxie blinked. He hadn't heard Lacoste's question when it had been asked a second before, but an echo of it now came back to him, something about distance off-shore. "How far offshore?" Maxie hazarded.

"Your man reports the twelve-mile line, but out here at night the line is hard to know."

"That I can see."

"Unless you say no, I start the zigzag."

"Right. Good." Maxie nodded and turned to look out the side port of the wheelhouse. The waves were flashing past like hasty ghosts, faint and rushed.

He wondered if the truth would ever come out about the mobs. Probably by the time it did, it couldn't possibly hurt them. Booze was only one line now. Funny how easy it was to start moving other lines once you got your organization organized.

From unloading the distillers' inventory, the boys created a thirst more powerful than the one that had been there before Prohibition. And once the good stuff from Kentucky was gone, it was back to the alky cookers and off to the smugglers to keep America from running dry. Once you mastered smuggling, you could smuggle anything, couldn't you?

Maxie blinked again. He knew it was way past the moment when he could afford the time to think about stuff like this. They were closing on the rendezvous point, couldn't miss it the way Lacoste was zigzagging over the area.

Back in Brooklyn Maxie had gotten a reputation for thinking. He was not happy about being tagged that way. At his age and station in life it was best if you looked like a good soldier and nothing else. That way, they handed you Suffolk County to operate. It didn't do you any good to be known as a smart-ass. Bright, yes. But always thinking, no.

Maxie nodded to Lacoste and turned to leave the wheelhouse. "I gotta round up my Marines with the choppers," he said. "Raise hell if you spot the rendezvous."

"*Mais certainement.*"

Maxie ducked down the ladder into the ready room. "On deck," he shouted to the machine gunners. "We're moving in fast. Take extra ammo drums along. You'll need 'em."

Chapter 18

The beach buggy jounced over the loose hillocks of sand. Heydt steered it closer to the strand, where the ocean crashed and collapsed in a surf so thick he could see its creamy line much farther than the dim headlights of the beach buggy shone.

It was a sorry excuse for a Coast Guard vehicle, something a few of the boys had put together in their spare time more for their own off-duty pleasure than for official business. But, having seen it, Ashley had commandeered it for patrol duty even though it wasn't C.G. property.

It had started, Heydt believed, as an abandoned Kissel or Locomobile sedan. But most of the original chassis had rusted away in the salty air of the beach. What was left was a fairly longish X-braced frame with good springs and axles into which the boys had put an air-cooled engine from a 1919 Franklin and a padded plank for a seat.

There was no windshield, no roof, but the dashboard

speedometer still worked fitfully, as did the immense headlamps, salvaged from a Duesenberg. As Heydt headed down onto the firmer, smoother sand that stretched along the surf, slick with sea water, the speedometer showed a good fourteen miles an hour. At that speed, Heydt figured, he was almost at Ocean Beach and well on his way to Point O' Woods and beyond.

He glanced to the left as he guided the beach buggy east along the strand. One house was lighted, its big square windows ablaze. From its position, he reckoned it to be the one that belonged to the chorine or whatever she was that Regan was currently laying the blocks to.

He glanced right at the ocean, trying to make out any signs of Ashley's patrol. Five minutes after they'd cast off on their silly mission, Heydt had jumped into the beach buggy and left the station in the command of Spanier, who knew what was going on. The other radio-man wasn't to be trusted with knowledge. But he was certainly to be trusted not to ask questions and to keep his big mouth shut.

Heydt could see the beginnings of the Point O' Woods settlement coming up on his left. At this time of the year no one lived there but caretakers. The dark, angular lines of the two- and three-story shingled houses formed a blacker jagged line against the sky. For a moment the scud over the moon parted, just long enough for Heydt to steer the beach buggy inland over the sand, the vehicle bucking and jouncing under him like a frightened horse.

He found the notch in the crest of the dune that led

into the Sunken Forest, but the beach buggy failed to make it up the sharp grade on the first run. Heydt backed her almost to the water's edge, then shoved the ancient transmission into low gear, advanced the gas feed very slightly, and started her forward, gears whining.

He managed to ram her up over the crest before her momentum gave out. Then he reduced the gas mixture to normal and gently fed torque to the rear axle. The beach buggy ghosted silently down the back slope of the dune in a sideways, crablike motion that brought it to the cottage in a few moments.

Heydt killed the engine, jumped out of the buggy, and strode loudly across the front porch. He hammered at the door. After a moment, Ellen Purvis opened it slightly, leaving the inside chain hooked in place.

"Oh, it's you," she said. "I thought—"

"Sure you did," Heydt assured her, his face expressionless. Behind her he could hear music playing.

She closed the door to unlatch the chain, then reopened the door and let Heydt in. "What brings you out on a night like th—"

Heydt cracked her hard across the mouth with the palm of his right hand. Ellen staggered, almost losing her balance. Her hand went to the blood rilling up over her lower lip. She touched it and stared at her reddened finger. "What are y—"

Heydt backhanded her in the other direction and this time she slumped to the floor. He rolled her over, crossed her wrists, and knotted a length of three-eighth-inch

Manila line about them. The Victrola continued to grind out band music.

"On your feet," he said, getting up.

Ellen got to her knees. Her mouth was pressed in a thin line, as if to keep blood from oozing out. Her eyes asked Heydt all sorts of questions, but he knew she was too afraid of him now to say anything more. She stumbled to her feet.

"Out," he ordered.

He led her to the beach buggy, sat her on the front seat, and lashed her ankles to the floorboards. Then he returned to the house. "S'wonderful," the woman on the phonograph record was singing, "s'marvelous. You could care for me."

The wind was from the east at the moment. Heydt picked up a kerosene lamp and smashed it against the east wall of the cottage. Then he struck a match and threw it into the pool of oil. The fire caught instantly with a thudding whoof.

". . . made my life so glamorous, you can't blame me for feeling . . ."

Heydt kicked out a window on the east wall and the wind started to spread the blaze over the rag rug. Flames licked at the Victrola.

Heydt left the front door open and ran for the beach buggy. He whipped the starter crank once and the hot Franklin engine caught immediately.

"You—you set a fire?" Ellen asked, her voice rising like a scream.

Heydt reversed the beach buggy in a tight arc, then shifted into low and started up the grassy back of the dune over the notch to the beach again. He had another four or five miles to cover farther to the east. Then he had to finish off the job and get back a good sixteen miles to the Coast Guard station in time to greet the returning heroes.

Chapter 19

The warmed-over tea tasted like ink, Maeve decided. She sat there in her nightgown and patched flannel robe, sipping the too-strong brew. She had never been one for reading, but tonight she desperately wished for something to take her mind off her thoughts.

She had no clear idea what time it was. Their only timepiece was Harry's wristwatch, which he had with him. She felt that, by now, he must have met the freighter and started unloading. Maybe he was finished and coming back.

She missed him badly at all times, but most when he was off on the smuggling business. Funny sort of business for a spoiled priest.

Maeve gave up the evil-tasting tea and poured the rest down the drain, leaves and all. She pumped some fresh water into the sink to flush away the leaves. Then, gathering her robe about her throat, she sat down in the rocker and tried to interest herself in the sewing she had earlier put away.

It was to be a dress for her, a fancy one of bright green printed cotton. She'd cut the skirt quite short, a regular flapper hemline, because she knew her legs were good, but the way she always dressed no one could possibly have guessed.

She held up the half-finished dress. Where in God's name would she be wearing such a thing? Would she and Harry ever have a life away from this island?

She supposed that to someone else Harry's life was a grand adventure. From the outside, looking in, it would seem that way, with its secrets and its stealth. Since that day in Ireland—1922, was it?—he'd gone almost anywhere trouble could be found and done almost anything that might get him into trouble. That, she supposed, was called adventure.

But it seemed to her that when he'd choked his comrade to death, the running had started and never stopped. This past year on the beach with her had been the longest he'd ever spent in one place since he'd fled Ireland.

Foolish for a man to be running from something lodged inside him like a bone in his throat. Maeve let the dress drop to the floor beside her. She stared down at the bright pool of green at her feet.

Green for Ireland. Her mouth twisted in a bitter half smile. Ireland had given his priest's dream a place to grow. And die.

There were so many places in the world now where a

man with that kind of dream could find himself a rousing fight. Harry had tried a few, Maeve knew, but never with the same pure virginal trust he'd placed in Ireland's cause. He'd never again put that much of himself on the line for anything. You only lost your maidenhead once.

Maeve found herself wondering when it was that Harry had first learned there was money to be made out of the betrayed dream? Somewhere in Latin America? It had come to him that there was gold in selling the guns other men wanted, needed, to win their dream of salvation.

Maybe she was being too harsh on the man. For the past year it hadn't been the money at all. It had been something else. Over the I.R.A. grapevine he'd heard that Dev's men had exonerated him. The strangling had been understood, finally, as a case of self-defense. And now, if he wanted it, there was an assignment for him.

She stared down at the puddle of green on the floor. It wasn't true that blood red was the strongest color. God, they'd read Harry's soul most cunningly, hadn't they? Someone back there had understood just what was eating at his innards. Someone knew him that well. And green was the color.

Green for redemption. Green for the virgin spring that banishes the winter's death. Green for the salvation of Harry Regan's poor, bloody soul.

This year on the beach, what was it but a penance? What would it gain him but his dream, whole and pure again? She could feel the tears start behind her lower lids. She blinked. They spilled up over her lashes and down her cheeks.

It was May and the bushes and shrubs of Fire Island were turning green. If only he would live through this night!

Chapter 20

The launch was a narrow, clinker-built, double-ended affair that the Coast Guard had bought back in the 1890's for surf rescues. Ashley hated that part of the service, the slowness, the stinginess, the cheapness of everything. He still hadn't heard back on his requisition for horses.

Now, as he crouched in the bow of the launch, Ashley wondered, as he had begun to do lately, whether the Coast Guard was really the place for him.

In one way, of course, he could think of no other place in the world that gave him rank, position, power, and a nearness to the sea. He didn't think of it in exactly those terms. He tended to think in terms of responsibility and service. But what it all boiled down to, he knew, was the good feeling of being permanently niched into a protected haven in this mean, hostile world.

He tended to think of the world, even in daylight, even

in sun under a clear sky, as being like the dark, dangerous night about him now.

The launch's bow hissed spitefully as it cleft the water. Now and then Ashley's face was drenched with salt water. Ahead he could see the patrol cutter with nothing showing but its red and green running lights. He had decided to trust to luck as far as the moon was concerned. Regan's luck had to give out some time. If the cloud cover had favored the rumrunner up till now, maybe it was Ashley's turn for a bit of luck when the time came.

Ashley's luck. He clung to the acetylene searchlight on the bow as the launch shot up over a high wave and plowed down into the trough behind it.

Ashley's only luck, he reflected, was to hang on. Hang on to the Coast Guard. Never mind the terrible thing in his gut. He would have it looked after one of these days when he could afford to take some of his leave time.

He had always been afraid to take his leave when it was due. He'd collected almost a month's extra leave time over the past two years by not taking it when he should. Perhaps one of these months he might just take the terrible risk and go away to some place where he wasn't known. Some good hospital, Johns Hopkins down in Baltimore maybe, and check in under a fake name and let them do whatever they had to do for the colitis. Operate. Cut. Whatever it took to rid him of the hot glowing coals in his gut.

The wind had quickened again. Ashley could hear it begin to whistle in the wire shrouds that braced the tiny mast the launch carried. He glanced back at his sharp-shooter crew. He had placed three of them on the starboard gunwale and two on the port side. The steersman was expected to stay with his tiller, no matter what.

Ashley saw that while the wind had grown stronger, they were in a fairly open stretch free of big waves. He clanged shut the steel signal shutters of the searchlight, reached inside and pumped up pressure, then released liquid into the calcium carbide generator. Shielding against the wind with his body, Ashley struck a match to the escaping acetylene jet. It flared bright yellow. He closed the ignition port and let the light burn away inside, hidden by steel plates from showing itself to the world outside.

The hostile world, Ashley thought. Hostile for me. Even more so for Regan. To be alone on the enemy ocean and suddenly to have the piercing beam of the acetylene searchlight prong through one like a bolt of colitis. He smiled.

The meanness of the world cut two ways, didn't it? One had to protect oneself against its hostility, but one could also focus some of the terror on others and, by so doing, protect oneself even more effectively.

If he captured Regan it might even mean a promotion. It would certainly stop anyone from a court-martial about his own drinking and that buried case of Dewar's in the dune.

He stared ahead at the cutter's red starboard running

light. It seemed to him that the launch was falling back. He turned to his steersman.

"Can you open her up any faster?"

"Aye, aye, sir."

Ashley heard the tired engine under the boxlike hatch begin to make a higher, more urgent sound. The launch sprang ahead as if released from a starting gate. In a moment it was abaft the cutter's stern. The launch's steersman guided the smaller craft alongside the cutter.

"Ahoy, the cutter," Ashley called, cupping his hands around his lips.

He saw Jorgensen's white cap in the darkness. "Ahoy, the launch."

"Increase speed one knot."

"Aye, aye, sir."

The white cap disappeared. After a moment Ashley was pleased to see the cutter begin to pull away from his launch again.

With any luck, he thought, he would soon be making Harry Regan feel the meanness of an exceedingly nasty world.

Chapter 21

Jim Purvis's boat had yet to show up. Two others had joined the *Deirdre* and Harry could see some other shapes moving up in the darkness, but Purvis had evidently gone off course in the night. No telling how many of the flotilla he had led astray.

"Timmy," he muttered, indicating a direction almost due south, "if Purvis shows up on a correction course, he'll be coming from that quarter. Keep your eyes peeled sharp."

"*Achtung, ja ja.*"

Harry watched a third boat join him. Good. He had damned near half his little fleet on hand. The rest would soon show.

He reached under a tarp and drew out a long five-cell nickel-plated flashlight. He aimed it at the general direction of the freighter. At this distance and in this darkness, Harry had no positive way of identifying the ship, any more than it had of making sure who he was. But the general outline of the confrontation seemed to fit the bill of particulars both he and the freighter captain had come to expect.

He opened the latch on the flashlight button and quickly pressed off a short burst of light, a long one and two short ones again.

This was good enough as a starter. In the old Morse it was X, which stood for a rendezvous in the graphic code of the Organization. The proper response was H.

When no light showed on the freighter, Harry decided they hadn't spotted the *Deirdre* yet. He signaled the dot, dash, and two dots again. This time he got an answering four dots. He repeated his X and the freighter repeated its H.

There was no mistaking it now, H being the same in old and new Morse. Harry put the flashlight away and cut in the *Deirdre*'s driveshaft. He eased the throttle forward very slightly and the beamy boat surged toward the freighter.

As he closed with the ship, Harry could see activity on board. Men had begun to move about the decks on the double, shoving cases into rough piles. A cargo crane amidships lifted a giant rope net sling carrying a cube of eight cases and began to swing it slowly to a position over the port side of the freighter.

"Here them blind bastards are," Timmy remarked, pointing due south.

A tiny rift in the moon's cloud cover showed Purvis and

the rest of the flotilla moving in at reduced speed. Harry wigwagged them to steer behind the group of boats now lined up with the *Deirdre*.

Aboard the stubby freighter, its patched sides scabby with rust in the sudden moonlight, another cargo crane hitched up a load of cases and swung them to the starboard side, balancing the first load. The ship stood waiting.

Harry advanced the throttle. The wind had begun to moan slightly in the freighter's rigging and he could hear it as the *Deirdre* moved in under her cargo sling. Harry cut his engine. The crane lowered its burden onto the deck between him and the cuddy cabin. Harry pulled open the rope netting and he and Timmy quickly stowed the eight cases below. They moved out fast under the overhanging stern of the ship to come under the cargo sling on the opposite side.

Meanwhile, the first sling had been reloaded and was swinging out again to deposit another cube of eight cases into a new boat. Led by the *Deirdre*, the flotilla would continue to circle the freighter, pausing to take on more cases until each captain felt he had loaded to just below the danger point.

Since each boat had a different capacity, the circling maneuver had been devised to allow an individual boat to steer out of the pattern and stand away once its full load was aboard. The circular track also kept the small boats from sliding sideways into each other and damaging themselves. They had only to keep clear of the freighter's rusty sides, stay in a single-file line, and all would be well.

Harry guided the *Deirdre* in its slow roundabout path, trying to calculate how long the whole operation might take. If the wind held true without shifting and if the scud over the moon grew no clearer than this, with their current loading rate they'd have a hundred or more cases stowed in each ship within the next fifteen minutes and the first to be topped off could start back.

He knew that almost anything could spoil this estimate. The cloud cover could break completely and leave the freighter and the boats totally visible, in case anybody was out here looking. The wind could shift and interact with the shoreward thrust of the waves to produce a dangerous cross-chop that made the loading pattern impossible to hold.

Then, too, Harry figured, he had to allow for the possibility that Ashley had seen something and decided to stir himself. If so, the boats had best head for the Sunken Forest and unload over the beach. The rest could sail further east to Harry's cabin near Long Cove and unload there.

This meant that Harry had to get word to the trucks that the stuff wasn't being unloaded from the boats onto a mainland dock at, say Islip or Bay Shore. Instead, the trucks would have to wait while the cases were transferred across the beach and the empty boats returned, innocently, past the Coast Guard station to Great South Bay again. That would bring them to—Harry glanced at his watch and saw that it was half-past midnight—damned near four in the morning before they could reload on the bayside shore of Fire Island and ferry the stuff across the bay to the waiting trucks.

Harry decided that it wouldn't be such a bright idea to transship the booze this morning. Coast Guard and hijackers might be combing Great South Bay.

Wondering whether it might not be the best thought, after all, to try to brazen his way past the Coast Guard station and trust to his luck with the moon, Harry guided a third load of eight cases onto the deck and helped Timmy stow them in the cuddy.

The *Deirdre* didn't seem to show that she had, so far, taken on twenty-four cases of Dewar's. She could take fifty more, Harry knew, before he would begin to get fussy about the placement of each case. All in all, if he jettisoned most of the sandbag ballast, he knew the *Deirdre* could take almost two hundred cases.

He steered her under the stern of the freighter. The sea was beginning to roughen. The wind had veered slightly. Harry glanced at the moon. Its face beamed down brightly on him and his works.

He swore softly to himself.

Chapter 22

Heydt eased the beach buggy over the dune and dropped quietly down the sand toward the small cabin on the shore of Long Cove.

The bright moon showed him the copper wires Regan had strung from the cabin to a post some fifty feet away. Heydt and Spanier had often tried to zero in with their revolving directional antenna on this particular part of the beach, hoping that Regan used the aerial wires for transmitting. But they had never gotten a signal from this direction.

The wind had begun to scream softly in the blueberry bushes and hiss through the dune grass. There was no light in the cabin.

Heydt shut off the motor and untied Ellen Purvis's ankles. Blood from her mouth had made a wide line down her chin and neck. It looked black in the moonlight. The ropes around her ankles had chafed through the skin. She had been jounced around badly on the buggy's plank seat, unable to brace herself as Heydt had plunged head-long down the beach.

"Out."

"What's this place?"

"Get walking."

"Why did you burn my cottage?"

He kicked her in the back of her knees and she went face down in the sand. He dragged her to her feet. "Good enough answer?" he asked, shoving her toward the cabin.

When they got there he rapped quickly on the door. No light shone inside, but he heard a rustling noise under the wind's moan. "Who's there?" Maeve called from in-side.

"Coast Guard. Open up."

"The hell you say."

Heydt took hold of Ellen and shoved her heavily against the cabin door. It shook but failed to open. He stood back and launched a kick at the knob.

He heard a shot and ducked down onto the sand al-most at the same moment. A bullet hole opened up in the door about four feet up from the sill.

"That won't do you any good," he called. "Surrender and open up."

The second shot kicked sand in his face. Heydt ran in a crouch toward the beach buggy and returned a few moments later with a one-gallon can of gasoline.

He dashed around the back of the cabin to its east side and sloshed the liquid all over the board-and-batten wall.

He stood away from it and tried to strike a match and throw it onto the gasoline. The wind kept blowing out the flame. Finally, one match caught and the side of the house went up in a great sheet of orange-yellow.

Ellen had begun to scream something Heydt couldn't understand. He hadn't thought to carry a gun on an errand like this. That damned Maeve Curran, he knew her family, old-line smugglers from way back.

". . . don't shoot me," he heard Ellen screaming.

Heydt snaked his way through the tall dune grass around to the front of the house. Ellen Purvis was lying across the doorway. The door slowly opened from inside.

Maeve Curran stood there in her robe, the harsh wind off the ocean pressing its flannel against her sharp young breasts. The fire had eaten its way inside the cabin now. Past her, Heydt could see the immense radio receiver on its table. One leg was afire and breaking. The battery jars began to slide off as the table tilted.

Maeve's face looked wild. Her black hair whipped around her face. Heydt saw her glance down at Ellen.

". . . len Purvis," he heard the woman scream. "It's Chief Heydt. Out there somewhere."

"Heydt?"

"He burnt my place, too."

"Heydt?" Maeve screamed. "Where are you, you black-hearted son of a mother bitch?"

Heydt stood up slowly. "No cause for alarm. It's official business. Coast Guard business."

The revolver kicked in Maeve's hand and Heydt felt

the bullet enter his abdomen near the left hip. He noticed that it had made no sound at all. Nor did the bullet hurt very much. It had the force to kick him backward a foot. But he got to his feet and started toward the two women again.

The gun kicked once more, but Heydt felt nothing. There was a giant roaring in his ears. The wind whipped the fire to shattering fury. The flaming cabin outlined itself against the night sky. Maeve fired again, pointblank, at his chest and he pitched forward on top of her.

His big, heavy-knit body pinned down both women. The flicker of the flames came and went in Heydt's vision. Sometimes he saw nothing. Sometimes the flames were very clear.

The world was filled with a roaring and screaming of fire and wind. Heydt could feel the women trying to squirm out from under him. He began to get what seemed to be the biggest erection he had ever had as the bodies writhed under his.

The front wall of the cabin pitched forward on top of them and Heydt could smell his own hair burning. He saw patches of flame shoot up in Maeve's fine black curls. Then he saw nothing. There was no air to breathe.

After a while he heard nothing and he felt nothing. He had been in extremely good physical shape and it took him quite a while to die. Probably the women had been luckier.

Chapter 23

The *Deirdre* waddled like a duck in the moonlight. As the little boats settled deeper in the water under their growing load, the lightening freighter loomed higher above them and it took the cargo booms longer to lower their eight cases into each small craft.

Harry circled the bow of the ship and stood off from the circling flotilla. He had almost two hundred cases aboard the *Deirdre* and Timmy was busy now at the port gunwale, jettisoning ballast bags of sand to lighten the boat.

Harry put the *Deidre* in a slow tight circle off the bow of the freighter. He glanced at the moon and wondered how long the brightness would last. He checked the loading operation on both sides of the freighter and saw that it was going slower now, much slower. The men were tiring and the boats were more sluggish.

"Timmy," he muttered, "go starboard now and dump some sand off that side."

"*Jawohl, mein kapitan.*"

"Lay off the Heinie talk, you Gaelic clod."

Harry declutched the driveshaft and let the engines idle. The *Deirdre*'s momentum continued to spin her slowly in a circle. Then she stopped and drifted. The sea had calmed considerably. For that Harry Regan was grateful. Now, if the cover would scud over the moon again.

He saw a glare from the direction of shore. At that distance, just over the twelve-mile line, the low-lying beach of Fire Island couldn't really be seen. By day, Harry could spot the Ocean Beach water tower and the lighthouse near the Coast Guard station. Few other things could be seen even in clear daylight. But something was burning on the beach.

He thought of the old days when the wreckers had lured ships to their death with false fires. People like Ashley's great-grandfather, maybe, or Jim Purvis's or Ellen's had been responsible for misleading dozens of sailing ships into the deadly surf.

Most likely it was a few folk, Harry thought, having themselves a beach barbecue. It was easy enough. They dug a pit, hardly a foot deep, and filled it with fast burning driftwood. The flames were always bright yellow along the beach because salt had gotten into everything, driftwood and logs alike.

As he watched, Harry saw another blaze much farther east. He frowned. Nobody lived that far away except a few squatters like himself. He discarded the picnic theory. It was one a.m. and no native went to bed much later than nine or ten at night. Most likely it was a house on fire. But two of them?

He wondered if Maeve were all right. He hadn't actually thought of her at all since he'd left her earlier in the evening. He rarely thought of a woman when he wasn't with her. Maeve was a wild sort of girl, too young for the life with him, but he enjoyed her.

Harry watched Timmy jettisoning sand bags. He wondered what kind of relationship he had with this burnt-out, drunk-up nobody. Anything more than he had with Maeve? Or Goldie, or Ellen, or any of the others? Harry knew he wasn't in a business that made for lasting relationships. But that was just an excuse, wasn't it?

And, for that matter, he wondered, what the hell sort of business was he in, anyway? The Sinn Fein business? The I.R.A.? Sure, he'd help the poor beggars out. Any Irishman with a heart would do the same. But maybe it was the other way around.

Maybe, Harry thought, I love this silly life so much I weave great intricate excuses for living it. But did it matter? Did anything matter but being free to do any of it? Or turn your back on it? To do what you goddamned well pleased without anyone to answer to or anyone to tell you no?

A brilliant star shell arched high into the sky. The magnesium flare turned the whole freighter, with its escort of circling boats, into a bluish-white snapshot.

An instant later two machine guns opened fire, raking sideways across the starboard flank of the freighter. Harry watched the bullets chop off Jim Purvis just below the chin. His head canted sideways, hanging by some sinews, as blood pumped up through the stump of his neck in a purplish froth under the cruel blue of the star shell.

Harry fell to the *Deirdre*'s deck and steadied the 9 mm. Parabellum on the gunwale. He could see the other ship quite clearly. It was about half the size of the freighter, some kind of converted government boat, but the Coast Guard didn't use choppers.

The star shell was beginning to die as it fell. Someone aboard the enemy ship turned on a massive searchlight. Harry held the Parabellum with both hands and put two slugs into the brilliant white eye. It went dark.

He got off another three rounds into the man who had turned on the light. The man lifted up on his toes and slowly jackknifed over the railing of the ship into the water.

"Get down, Timmy," Harry shouted.

He kicked in the clutch and shot the *Deirdre* forward around the port side of the freighter, shielding himself from the enemy ship. "What the hell boat is that?" he yelled.

"Corvette," Timmy shouted back. "Hijackers." His voice was trembling with excitement. "Hot damn."

Harry watched Timmy unsling the Thompson and crouch down behind the *Deirdre*'s gunwales for safety. "I'm going to come out slowly off the freighter's stern," Harry said. "When I do, give the corvette everything you can, Timmy."

"Aye, aye."

Harry eased the gasoline feed to trolling speed and the *Deirdre* crept slowly along the scaley flank of the freighter. He could hear a rattle of small arms fire above his head as the ship's crew began firing on the corvette. The deeper coughing sound of heavy machine-gun fire was slower and more deliberate than the yapping bark of the hand guns.

The sweet stench of cordite filled his nose. Harry gently eased the *Deirdre* out of the shadow of the freighter and saw that the corvette was standing away from the freigher, concentrating its fire on the little boats of the flotilla.

Harry sighted along the Parabellum's barrel at the corvette's wheelhouse. So far no one had seen him. Behind the wheel he could make out a short man with a shadowed face, as if he wore a beard or needed a shave. Harry put a careful shot into the face and missed. They saw him now.

He could see chopper fire spitting across the waves toward him as the gunner tried to hold down the barrel and keep his shots from skying.

Harry reversed the driveshaft of the *Deirdre*. As the boat stopped and began to move back out of sight of the corvette, he put two more shots into the wheelhouse and saw the man at the wheel disappear. The ship began to turn aimlessly. Someone else grabbed the spokes and twirled them to get the corvette back in control.

"You didn't give me no chance, Harry."

"Sorry. They'll expect us to pop out off the bow of the freighter this time. We'll appear at the stern. Don't start firing till I get me one or two of them."

He reversed the driveshaft once more and gave the *Deirdre* a strong jolt of gas. She came surging out of the safety of the freighter at a good five knots. Harry quickly picked off a gunner working the fixed .50 watercooled machine gun he had heard before.

Timmy opened up with the Thompson. He used it stiffly, but well, ticking off bursts of three and four. Harry saw that, while the slugs were hitting the corvette, they did no damage to her plate-steel hull. They had the effect however, of forcing the enemy to take cover.

Harry took a moment to check on his flotilla. He could see four of the boats drifting out of the loading circle and assumed the men aboard had been shot. The rest had probably run for cover. He could see two of them inching in behind the freighter. Half the shipment, at least, was kaput.

He rammed the gas feed full on. "Give it to 'em, Timmy!" he shouted. He pulled the tiller hard to one side and sent the *Deirdre* lumbering at her top speed toward the corvette. From time to time Harry zigzagged but the corvette was less than a hundred yards from him now and evasive action wouldn't do the trick.

Timmy's submachine gun rattled harshly, no longer trying to save rounds. He was pouring a steady stream of slugs across the corvette's deck. Harry could see sparks where the bullets hit steel.

He reached under the engine hatch and came up with two hand grenades. He held one in each hand, pulled the rings with his teeth and held down the timing levers.

The *Deirdre* was racing wildly at the corvette, barely twenty yards away. Timmy's barrage kept the deck clear for a moment. Harry touched the tiller and sent his boat on a course that would scrape alongside the ship.

He cocked his right arm back and let one grenade fly through the air. As it tumbled end over end, he switched the other grenade to his right hand. So near were the two craft now that he could lob the second grenade over the corvette's railing. He watched it bounce on the deck and roll down a gangway.

He veered the *Deirdre* off sharply on a tangent and had her ten yards off the corvette's stern when the first grenade exploded. He turned back as the second grenade went off deep in the bowels of the corvette. That was why he got the slug in the chest, rather than the back.

Chapter 24

There had never been any doubt in Maxie's mind that they would pull this off. They had everything—more men, faster boat, more guns, heavier firepower, and the ace in the hole, surprise.

When he fired the star shell the whole thing became as clear as day, the little boats scuttling for cover like cockroaches when you stepped on them. The monkeys aboard the freighter had nothing heavier to throw at them than .32 and .38 slugs from six-shot revolvers.

Only that bastard Regan in his low-lying boat, the one that showed hardly any profile above the water, only that boat and the bastard who ran her gave Maxie any real trouble. He had sized it all up in a few moments. He was good that way, good and experienced.

In a fight like this nobody wanted to get killed. You took the fight out of the turdkickers who were unloading the boat by showing them what a chopper could do to a man. That calmed them all down nice.

Only the bastard playing hide-and-seek on the other side of the freighter gave him trouble. Maxie assumed he had to be Regan. Fine. He knew where Regan was but Regan didn't know who or where Maxie was. Perfect.

When Regan's sharpshooting put the Frog captain out of commission, Maxie had grabbed the wheel in time. He tried to mobilize his two chopper men, but one of them was reloading and the other had been taken out by a bullet from that funny-looking gun of Regan's.

Now the bastard was coming at him with that flying scow. There was nothing to shoot at, damn it. The thing lay so low to the water you couldn't really put a burst into her.

Some boob with a chopper was trying to make Swiss cheese out of the corvette's steel. Maxie grinned and reached for the over-under shotgun the captain, Lacoste, usually kept next to the wheel. The low-slung boat was almost on him now.

Maxie saw Regan stand up and chuck a grenade, then another. There was a taste of brass and blood at the back of Maxie's mouth. He tried to take careful aim as the boat sped away from him. This son-of-a-bitch would queer the whole thing. He had to be gotten out of the way. The first grenade went off, throwing Maxie to the deck.

He scrambled to his feet and fired both barrels as the second grenade went off. The whole corvette shuddered.

It wasn't possible, Maxie told himself. Two grenades

couldn't do it. But Regan would be back to try again. If he wasn't put out of the way, he would, all by himself, ruin Maxie's entire job.

Maxie grabbed the wheel and started to play with the controls he had watched Lacoste using. This thing on the right was for speed. Maxie shoved the control all the way forward. The engines below responded and the bow of the corvette surged up in the air as it began to move forward. Good. The grenade hadn't spoiled anything yet.

Maxie hauled the wheel hard port and forced the corvette to turn almost in her own length. He pointed her dead on Regan's boat. He could see the bastard crouching in the stern. Or lying there. He couldn't tell. He would ram the son-of-a-bitch and put him out of the way for good.

Maxie tried to shove the throttle harder ahead but there was no more play in the speed control. The corvette was moving as fast as she could and closing the gap every second. Beneath him, Maxie could hear wild thrashings and heavy knocks, as if something big had broken loose and was rumbling about in the hold.

He watched Regan turn over on his stomach. Didn't matter, bastard, Maxie thought. Either way you get it you get it for good.

At that moment another star shell shot skyward with a whistling hiss. The flare was almost blinding. Maxie winced and turned to glance over his shoulder.

A Coast Guard launch was closing on his starboard quarter, the swabbies letting off a fusillade of rifle fire.

They picked off his chopper man. Behind the launch, Maxie could see a cutter bearing down at him at a slightly different angle.

Maxie yanked the wheel hard port and put the corvette in another tight turn. The steel bow almost absentmindedly left a gash in the stern of Regan's boat. The impact made Regan roll on his side, but Maxie had stopped watching him now and was trying to outrun the Coast Guard.

We are pre-eminently the world's most excessive and violent of peoples. Must even our most breathtaking achievements remain both excessive and violent? Witness the outrageous hubris with which Lindbergh locked himself in lone mortal combat, throttling the elements into submission. What becomes of us when even this last frontier is gone and every ocean, every sky, is tamed? Will then our irrational bent toward violence ferment disastrously within us and, flowing like an angry red tide, drown us in our own nature? What has happened to us, the last great hope of a perfect society?

E. Channing Holmes
(as quoted in the N.Y. *Times*,
July 11, 1927)

Chapter 25

"It couldn't have been anything but gunfire," Goldie said. She ran her fingers through her tough blonde hair and glared out the living room window at the unresponsive night.

"Thunder," Paul Lachaise suggested.

"Balls."

He had stopped drinking some time ago because each sip of whisky, instead of putting him out, had seemed to make everything much too clear. He was getting sick, not with the nausea of dizziness, but with something deeper and worse that frightened him.

Goldie turned back to look at him. Her white pajamas twisted loosely along with her thin body, coming to rest slightly after she had. "You okay, Paul?"

He nodded. "Regan isn't."

Her mouth tightened. "He's okay. He has more lives than . . ." She turned back to the window. "Ocean's getting rougher. Did you see that big burst of light before? There's a hell of a battle going on out there somewhere."

Paul sat up straighter. He tried to master the sickness but it was unlike anything booze had ever done to him before. God knew, he told himself, with the rotgut he'd guzzled in his time, too much of even the real thing shouldn't do him in this way. It was as if he had given up something, or was about to. Not vomited it, he noted, but had it torn from him by main force. Having a baby delivered? He winced.

"This is always the trouble," Goldie said, sighing impatiently at the window. "When you have a romance going with a bum like Regan, you never know when he'll come back to you. Or in what shape. Or even if."

"Don't call him a bum," Lachaise said. His voice sounded odd and wild to him. He started to get out of the wicker sofa. "He's a gentleman."

"When you say that, smile."

"He is." Lachaise felt his body settle back heavily, like the weight of a fat old man. Something big and ugly and unwieldy seemed to be stirring inside him and it wasn't the whisky. Had he ever felt this way before? "Maybe once before," he said aloud.

"What?"

"At Ypres. Once before at Ypres." He pronounced it as the Tommies did—"Wipers"—and merely saying the word seemed to make him much sicker.

"You?" Goldie eyed him curiously. "When?"

"Oh, not when the poor dumb bastards walked into the

gas attack. That was 1915." He tried to summon up the memory without deepening the sick feeling. "This was later. My outfit came through Ypres in '17, after Passchendaele."

"You? In Belgium?"

"Goddamn it." This time he managed to stand up. "I was over there and you bloody well know it."

She went to him. He was fascinated by the way her long, loose crepe de chine pajama trousers seemed to flow with a separate life of their own. He felt her pressing down on his shoulders, gently. He let her ease him back down on the sofa. "I didn't mean it that way, honey," she said.

He stared at the smoldering butt of a Murad he had left in the abalone-shell ashtray. "The gas was all gone, of course," he said, mostly to himself. "Chlorine? Phosgene? It's so long ago. Does anybody remember? But the lousy Belgians had never cleaned up Ypres properly. The Tommies had carried off their wounded and most of their dead, but they'd been on the run, you see, so they couldn't take all the bodies with them. And the bloody Belgians just left the bodies lying there. The gas did something horrible to the flesh after a while. And then, later, to the bones. This was two years later and the Belgians still hadn't touched them. Hardly blame them, I suppose. Dead men, skeletons, mostly. Yellowish-green men. Superputrefaction. But we had fresh dead. Haig butchered half a million there in the summer and fall of '17. We had death in every stage. A museum of death. Two-year old corpses. Six-month corpses. The fresh ones were the worst. The month-old ones. Super-putrefaction. Eyeballs hanging out on strings."

He stood up again, turned blindly, and ran out of the room. He made it to the bathroom, but not to the sink.

He lay on the tile floor, trying to edge away from his own puke. The cold white tiles were hexagonal, forming rosettes with hexagonal black centers. The pattern repeated once every foot. The sharp edges of the tiles cut at his cheek. He arched sideways away from the vomit, trying to escape it and, in his bewilderment, it seemed to surge toward him like a living thing.

He could hear Goldie coming up behind him. "Paul. My God, what a mess. Paul?"

He closed his eyes, and in a moment he was asleep.

Chapter 26

It was always the same, Ashley told himself. They had the faster boats, bigger ships, more powerful engines, heavier armament. So, of course, Regan's corvette had outrun both the Coast Guard cutter and the launch in which Ashley sat crouched, like a carved figurehead, slowly raking the sea ahead of him with the blinding yellow of the acetylene searchlight.

No, it really wasn't much of a job in the Coast Guard, he mused. There seemed nothing in it any more a man could rely on.

Even the freighter had disappeared. As riddled as she had been, she had apparently set course straight out to sea. By the time Ashley's boats had given up chasing the corvette and returned to the freighter, her scaly hulk was gone. Even when the moon came out, neither Ashley nor Ensign Jorgensen had been able to see any sign of the ship out to sea.

The other small boats had scattered, too. It had been a naval battle with ghosts, nothing but ghosts. The only two ships he could actually swear to were his own.

The yellow beam raked across something and continued on its way. Ashley sat up and slowly moved the beam back. It illuminated an inboard boat whose cabin had been half shot away.

"Ahead slow," Ashley called to his steersman.

The launch slowed. It closed with the drifting boat. In the rising seas, the boat seemed almost entirely beneath water, only the oval outline of its gunwales and cabin above the waves. Some inner buoyancy was holding it up for a few last moments. Ashley could see someone bending over the tiller. As the launch drew closer, he realized the man had no head. His body had somehow gotten wedged between the jammed tiller and the stern.

"Take it in tow, sir?" one of the men asked.

Ashley frowned. The last thing he wanted was to turn this expedition into a towing operation, hauling back the spoiled carcass of some luckless rumrunner.

"He's dead," Ashley said.

"But, I—"

"Very well." Ashley realized that the usual mealy-mouthed morality they all lived by required some kind of Christian burial.

As bowsman, it fell to him to ship a line around a cleat that stuck up above the waves. He paid out a few yards of line and then made it fast to the launch's starboard gunwale. "Half speed ahead."

"Aye, aye, sir."

Poor, headless dummy, Ashley thought. It could even be Regan, for all anyone knew. That he should end up this way. The world was hard and mean. One couldn't ever go it alone. One had to niche himself into something where he could feel secure from the world. Eccentrics like Regan had no place any more. In the future, one either had one's niche in something bigger, one's safe berth in an organized way of life, or one had to die for it. Alone, headless, nameless, unmasked.

The minute a forward motion was given to the wrecked boat, it began to sink and Ashley had only a few seconds to free his end of the line before the other boat went to the bottom. The men stared unhappily at where the boat had been.

"We wouldn't even have known who he was," Ashley said. He knew he was speaking mostly for his own benefit. The ignorant men would have been as self-congratulatory burying a headless corpse as any other kind. It was the form of Christianity, not the matter, that counted.

Yet it irked him not to know who the criminal was. "Did any of you see a name on the boat?"

He listened to the chorus of "no, sir" and resumed sweeping the waves with the searchlight. It could have been Regan, himself. But, no, Regan would have been aboard the flagship, that fast corvette. In other words, Regan had given him the slip again.

The pain in his colon kindled abruptly. In the excitement of surprising the rumrunners, he had forgotten the pain. Or else it had gone away. Now it was back and he had neither aspirin nor whisky to fight it with.

Suddenly the acetylene searchlight went dark. Ashley burned his fingers prying open the side. He delved into the carbide container. Empty, used up.

He sat back in the bow and considered his alternatives. The moon had dropped to the horizon now. Dawn would be along in a few hours at the most. He guessed he was no more than a mile or two offshore and, what with the zigzagging they had done, no more than five miles east of Cherry Grove. He could begin to head back now by compass and pick up a little light as he went along. He'd be back at the station by sunup.

With nothing to show for the night but a length of line lost and a run-down acetylene searchlight.

Out of the corner of his eye he caught a faint flicker of light in the direction of land. He turned to face it directly and there was nothing to see. But, again the Coast Guard had taught him about the increased sensitivity of, what did they call it, peripheral vision. You could better see fainter things sideways than dead ahead. He held the night glasses to his eyes and slowly swung them across where he conceived the shoreline would be.

That was when he caught sight of the flames.

Chapter 27

Regan had been trying for some time to claw the black wool sweater away from the wound. Although it was too dark to see, he kept wanting to examine the hole in his chest. He wanted to see what kind of chance he had.

The wind was rising again. The *Deirdre* was running at top speed but Harry Regan had no idea how long she had been running or in what direction. His left hand kept pulling at the knitted wool. The sweater gave way with insidious smoothness but refused to part.

He had tried to reach the wound with his other hand, but his right arm was twisted under him in some peculiar way. He decided he would have to roll himself over to free his right hand.

He braced his left elbow against a cleat on the thwart and with all his strength began to lever himself sideways. His arm trembled wildly. The pain in his chest grew suddenly worse. He persisted for a few seconds more and finally was able to roll his body over on his back.

He lay there, gasping for breath, somehow feeling that this would ease the pain he had stirred up inside him. Then he reached for the throttle control and cut the engine to an idle.

"Timmy?"

The wind slapped the word away from him. He had no strength to shout and he knew that, as he was now, his voice couldn't carry as far as the cuddy cabin where Timmy might be. A faint stink of whisky seemed to rise from the floorboards, a sweet, malty smell that reminded him of Timmy. He was staring up at the moon. The low-lying cloud cover had all but closed in again. Somehow, he felt, the wind had changed quarter. He had been unconscious for a while, but there was something changed about the relation of the sea and the wind that he could feel.

Harry thought about the way the wind had been veering all evening. He wished he had paid more attention to the pattern of its movement. It meant something and he wished he knew the meaning.

He levered himself sideways and tried to find the little hand compass he normally used. It was good enough for rough navigation and to get you out of a thick fog. The shaking movement of his arm quickened the pain. He tightened his jaw against it.

But the pain worried him, the severity of it and his

ignorance of the wound. He reached down to the bottom of the sweater and the shirt beneath it. He pulled them both up high over his nipples and twisted his head to look at the wound.

It had to be somewhere near his right nipple because most of the pain was centered there. Some of it shot up and down his right side with each pitch and yaw of the *Deirdre,* drifting now with an idling engine. In the near darkness the blood lay sticky and black on his skin. He wished for a clear moon.

She had proved fickle tonight, hadn't she? The scudding cover had held at first, luring him to try his luck. Then she had quit him for someone else.

Harry wondered about luck. What happened when two men, each with his own luck, collided? He grinned in the dark. Regan, Ashley. He sighed. And some miserable dog-robbing bastard of a hijacker for a third man. Of them all, one's luck was holding, and it clearly wasn't Regan's.

Probably, he thought, I've tempted and taunted my poor luck and used it once too often without even a kind word for it. The poor, neglected thing was wore out just keeping my women from getting pregnant.

When he grinned again, the motion of his facial muscles stretched the skin of his neck enough to kindle the same fire in his breast once more. It was something, he thought, a bit more than a flesh wound, one might say. He remembered not to grin.

"Timmy?"

Poor, hapless no-good. But it was the excitement he wanted and got. Guns the Organization wanted. And money Purvis was after. And me, he thought, me?

What was it I was after that I'll now never get?

He had few illusions about his prowess as a sailor. Leading his Fire Islander men he was the one-eyed in the kingdom of the blind. But he knew no celestial navigation at all. The position of the moon and sun and stars told him nothing about his own progress. He was a sight-of-land sailor at best, although with a compass, a chronometer, and a good chart he could dead-reckon pretty respectably. Now, at night, off course, lost, wounded, the hunted quarry in an overloaded boat, he dead-reckoned his prospects as poor.

Harry rolled over a fraction more and scrabbled his fingers blindly about on the floor boards. He found and retrieved the old Luger and a spare magazine. He found a loose grenade. Then he located the flat cylinder of the compass. He set it down on the thwart near his face.

The *Deirdre* was pitching about more violently now. The seas seemed higher and more urgent. Harry squinted at the dial of the compass, but there was nothing to see except some tantalizing flickers of movement as the card wheeled and dipped with the motion of the boat.

The freshening wind chilled his chest, moist with blood. If and when the cloud cover parted over the moon he had so many, many things to look at. The compass, his wound. He had to get his bearings. Find Timmy. Put the

Deirdre shipshape. Set about the business of saving himself.

He touched his breast and found that the wound was sopping again. He seemed to be bleeding very freely. He registered this with an almost casual lack of concentration.

He could feel himself blacking out. There seemed to be nothing he could do about it.

Chapter 28

Maxie throttled back on the righthand controls. The corvette lost speed. He had been fairly sure, for the last ten minutes, that he had evaded both the Coast Guard cutter and launch. The noises below had quieted, too.

In fact, he told himself, I'm in pretty good shape for a guy who's fucked up completely.

He played around with the controls until he found a combination that seemed to give the least forward motion to the ship. By glancing from time to time at the compass binnacle in front of him, he was able to aim the corvette in a southeast direction he felt sure would not run him aground on anything. That it might take him too far from land for comfort was something he had decided to worry about later.

He attached the brass clamps to the steering wheel. Then he stepped over Lacoste's corpse, brushed past the dead radioman, and made his way out on deck.

The wet steel was slippery under his pointed shoes. He moved cautiously because the corvette was, for all its size, bobbing violently in a series of choppy waves that kept breaking over her side in long furrows.

He surveyed the damage where Regan's first grenade had gone off. Apparently it had done almost nothing to the steel plate except scorch it fiercely and engrave a neat star of outward radiating lines where the grenade body had fragmented into what amounted to shrapnel. It had been those bits of iron, however, that had done in Sparks and the ex-Marine gunner in the stern of the corvette.

Goddamn Regan, Maxie thought. He was beginning to feel in his gut what his too-bright brain had already told him. One man in a rotten garbage-scow hulk had laid waste the whole hijack. Against superior odds and planning, Regan had settled Maxie's hash, probably for good.

Maxie paused at the head of the aft ladder going down into the hold. For a moment he postponed actually seeing what he knew he would find.

If only Regan had been put out of action earlier! The arrival of the Coast Guard vessels had been nothing, in itself, that Maxie couldn't have handled. With his full crew and firepower, he could have lured the cutter and launch away from the scene, shot them up, and returned to loot the flotilla of small boats.

But by the time the swabbies had showed, Regan had already killed all of his men on deck and, Maxie felt sure, most of them waiting below to join the fracas.

He climbed down the ladder. Smoke spread in layers through the air. Maxie's lungs seemed starved. He inhaled, but the stink of the smoke caught in his throat. It wasn't the sweet nitrate smell of cordite or smokeless powder. Something had caught fire down here and burned. He glanced slowly around the hold.

Of the Dutchman's contingent of Long Island plowjockeys, Maxie saw, none seemed to be among the living any more. There had been a pack of them, husky blonde monkeys Maxie needed to reload the cases from Regan's small boats onto the corvette. Apparently the farmers had all been huddled in a frightened heap near the aft gangway when the grenade bounced into the hold.

The efficiency of Regan's attack on the corvette was now painfully clear. Even if the Coast Guard hadn't arrived, it would have been impossible to hijack the flotilla. There weren't enough of Heinckel's turdkickers left to unload a pod of peas.

Maxie slumped back against the steel bulkhead and cursed himself for not ramming Regan when he had the chance. He should never have let the two swabby ships distract him. Another second or two and the corvette could have plowed Regan under for good.

Now Maxie had nothing to show for the night's work but a lot of wasted ammo and enough dead ones to sour all the locals on working with him again. His principals back in Brooklyn would be very upset. It wasn't only the hijacked booze they required. In fact, Maxie knew, that was the least of it. A few bottles and some newly printed bogus labels and his bunch could always be peddling what they claimed to be Dewar's.

No. The big thing they wanted from Maxie was enforcement. Only the mob's boats should be able to land booze. Fire Island beaches were to be marked "Private, Keep Out" to free-lance bastards like Regan. It was as much Maxie's job as getting the booze to enforce the proposition that no one else be allowed to. Yes, Brooklyn was going to be upset. Of course, Regan had looked wounded at the last . . .

Maxie brightened up. He went into the aft hold and found two of his men still on their feet trying to patch up two of the rest.

"Drop it, Aldo," he snapped.

"He's bleedin'."

"Drop it." Maxie gestured sideways with his left hand as he ducked his right hand beneath his dark brown jacket. "Out of the way, Aldo."

He produced the seven-shot .32 Beretta automatic and put one slug into the head of the man Aldo had been working on. The flat crack echoed and rang in the steel room.

"Any more wounded?" he asked.

Aldo's eyes widened. He jerked his head sideways at another man who was painstakingly bandaging the head of a youth of eighteen. "Patsy," Maxie barked, "leave Kurtz alone. Stand aside."

Kurtz looked up at Maxie. "I'm okay, Maxie. Swear to God I'm okay."

Maxie shook his head. "No hard feelings, Larry." He opened a small black hole between Kurtz's eyes. "Any more?" he asked, turning to Aldo and Patsy. Their eyes crawled sideways toward the swinging door of the head. Maxie nodded. "Get busy and dump these two over the side. I'll have some fresh stiffs when you get back down."

He waited until they began lugging Kurtz's long, skinny body up the ladder. Then he stepped into the head. The urine-ammonia stench prickled in his nostrils. The rest of his boys, five of them, lay in odd positions. After they had been wounded they had evidently had barely enough strength to crawl in here for protection against further attacks. They shifted slightly now with the bobbing of the ship.

Maxie tried to guess how badly each was wounded. The two men he had killed outside had seemed in better shape than these, which was probably why Aldo and Patsy had decided to try getting them patched up and back in shape. But these five were worse than walking wounded. One man had a stomach hole. Another had lost part of his jaw.

Maxie emptied the Beretta carefully, with a certain peasant economy of purpose. It held seven cartridges and he had already used two. The remaining five dispatched the five wounded men.

The two men had finished heaving their dead comrades over the side and now appeared in the doorway of the head as if attracted by the shots. Aldo's eyes grew wider as he surveyed the damage.

"That's s-some shooting, Maxie," he managed to say.

"Each one between the eyes." Maxie grinned. "And back on Greenpoint Avenue, they don't even know me as Maxie the sharpshooter. This I learned from Uncle Sammy."

He and Aldo chuckled together. Maxie had been rummaging around in the pockets of his jacket for a fresh clip of bullets. He found it, checked it over. He yanked the spent clip from the Beretta's butt and shoved a fresh magazine into the automatic pistol.

"Now," he said, "I go kill me a Mick."

Chapter 29

It was the chill that, eventually, roused Harry Regan. The wind had whipped spray over his naked chest. The combination of salt, burning into the wound, together with the chill cold of his skin, pulled him back to the edge of consciousness.

He listened for a moment, trying to concentrate. Something was different. The engines had stopped. He'd run out of gas.

Then he saw that the clouds had parted over the moon. She rode right on the horizon now, but she still gave him light. He glanced at the compass card. The *Deirdre* was drifting almost due east, it seemed.

Depending on how long she had run her earlier course at full speed, and in what direction, she could be offshore anywhere from ten to fifty miles. Harry's first reaction was to sit up and do something about it.

But his weakness had made him cautious. He lay there and tried to think. The whisky smell was still strong around him but he knew there was no point in calling for Timmy. He began to touch his right breast very gingerly. It took some finding but he finally located a very small entry hole that felt almost round. He craned his neck to look at it. With its crust of scab, it resembled a brand new nipple an inch to the right of the old one.

He restrained himself from grimacing. He touched the hole again. The salt in the air and water had helped plug it up with a good-size clot. He hoped it would hold. He hoped he wouldn't break it free by moving too fast or too much.

In the cuddy he had a tin box with iodoform and court plasters. But getting there was something else.

Harry realized he was not only afraid to move too much, but he actually didn't have the strength to do much moving. He lay perfectly still with the wet thwart under his back. From time to time the wind dashed spray across his face and chest. He shivered with cold.

What could have put a small round hole in him? A slug from a rifle or chopper, he knew, tumbled end over end and, like as not, tore through you sideways. He remembered once in a Veracruz cantina during *huracán* weather. The barometer had dropped low enough to addle men's minds and one of his close drinking buddies had put a 303 slug into him from an old Mark III Lee-Enfield. It had gone in one side of his calf, making a sort of keyhole slot. It had torn its way out the other side carrying a few ounces of meat with it through an exit hole the diameter of a silver dollar.

Funny. He tried to breathe calmly and slowly to minimize the motion of his chest and keep the bloodclot in the wound from tearing loose. The longer he kept it there, he told himself, the more securely it would seat itself.

Funny wound, and no exit hole. Maybe he'd stopped a piece of shot. Maybe the hijacker had used a scattergun on him. If so, the pellet had to be 0 or 00 buckshot, almost as thick as a pencil and too damned slippery to get out easily with a probe or tweezers. In the tin box he had both. But he doubted he'd do any probing tonight.

His thoughts grew hazy. He wasn't blacking out, but he felt drowsy now and weak. If he fell asleep the *Deirdre* might continue drifting so far offshore that the Gulf Stream current could start her north toward Nova Scotia. Past Greenland. Back to the Hebrides with her load of whisky. Coals to bloody Newcastle. The wound had stopped hurting. He was in favor of that.

To nestle into Maeve's arms. She could be gentle. Ah, Christ, they all could if they'd a mind. And what did it cost them to give a man heartsease? And what was there in life, after all, except that? Giving it and getting it.

The *Deirdre* continued to drift sideways through a mounting sea. When she had turned enough abeam, the next wave broke amidships and sent freshets of seawater sluicing along the floorboards. The old boat shuddered. Her death was close at hand and she seemed to know it.

Another wave hit her full starboard and she shook with the impact. The cockpit floor was awash now as fresh sea-water shipped over the gunwales.

Harry sighed. He could feel the *Deirdre* yaw violently and creak with fear. He opened his eyes.

Slowly, trying not to strain loose the clot in his chest wound, he rolled sideways and sat up. His feet dangled in the swirling cockpit water. Half flooded, the *Deirdre* would founder with the next wave, or the one after that. She was wallowing now, as if in panic, yawing this way and that like a trapped animal, swerving deeper and more uncontrollably into disaster.

Harry worked the choke three times and whirled the magneto starter. The engines coughed into life. Maybe there was enough gas left to head her into the wind. He pulled the tiller hard port and the *Deirdre* responded by swinging slowly until she faced into the west. The spray whipped into Harry's eyes with blinding force. The engines sputtered and died.

Harry wondered if he had the strength to set a sail on the *Deirdre*'s stubby mast, just enough rag in this wind to give the boat way to steer by. He knew that in a few minutes the *Deirdre* would drift sideways again to the sea and the waves would start to swamp her. Loaded as she was, she would sink in seconds.

Harry groped for the nearest case of whisky. He pulled a loose board free. Nails groaned in the wind. He pulled up a bottle of Dewar's, held it to the moon, and saw the bullet hole in the clear glass that had drained the whisky.

He yanked out another bottle and twisted off the lead foil. He pried out the cork and held the bottle to his lips. The whisky surged out into his mouth. He swallowed twice, fast.

The alcohol carved a fiery line down his throat like a runnel of molten iron. It hit his stomach and he felt suddenly warm again. He swallowed twice more and went down on his knees. Crawling slowly so as not to strain his wound, he made his way forward to the cuddy.

The booze got me into this, he thought, and it'll damned well get me out. Maybe it would give him enough strength to heave over the anchor. Maybe his measly hundred feet of anchor hawser were enough to reach bottom. Maybe he could keep the *Deirdre* into the wind that way until he'd run up some kind of sail. Maybe.

The moon dipped into the horizon. It became, with chilling abruptness, a half moon. The *Deirdre* was drifting sideways into the smashing waves.

Maybe not, Harry thought.

Chapter 30

The cutter had already tied up in its mooring alongside the great wooden dock that ran from the Coast Guard station out into the bay. Lt. Ashley supervised the tying up of the launch and sent its crew inside to get some hot coffee and bunk down for a few hours.

The creosote smell of the dock was a homely reminder of land to Ashley. He wasn't all that sure he enjoyed cruising about the ocean in a craft not meant for ocean cruising. The sky was lighter now.

It had been an ungodly night. Zero as far as results were concerned. Ashley considered himself fortunate not to have lost any of his men, none of them even injured. Apparently Regan's corvette had been disabled even before Ashley had arrived. He wasn't sure what had happened to the rum fleet. Some mysterious falling out. No honor among . . .

"Sir?" Jorgensen asked.

Ashley turned to face the red-cheeked ensign, who was holding a salute. Ashley returned the gesture. "Report, Mister."

"Chief Heydt's not back yet from shore patrol in the beach buggy, but Spanier says—"

"Not back from what?"

"Didn't you tell him to . . ." Jorgensen's voice died away as he remembered more clearly what had happened before the launch and cutter had gone out. "But that's right," he said wonderingly. "You specifically told him not to send out a shore patrol."

Ashley nodded. "Your memory's improving, but not by much. Spanier still in the radio room?"

Jorgensen nodded. "He's pretty sleepy, sir. All the men are."

"So am I," Ashley snapped. "Pick six of your men for early watch and send the rest to their quarters to bunk down. Tell Spanier to report to me at my quarters in—" Ashley glanced at his wristwatch and found that it was almost five in the morning "—ten minutes. Dismissed."

Jorgensen snapped a salute again and, without waiting to have it returned, headed off along the wooden dock toward the station. Ashley grinned minimally, a gesture that only disturbed the corners of his mouth and slightly flattened his already thin lips. Now that Jorgensen had finally seen a little action, abortive and confusing though it was, he seemed to be shaping up into a much more willing and pliable flunky.

Ashley went to his room and switched off the hanging

electric bulb which he had left burning in the haste of departure. He swallowed three aspirin tablets with water. He knew the silver flask was empty, but he shook it next to his ear anyway and heard a faint, tiny noise. He let a bit of water drip into the flask, swished it around, and swallowed it. The water tasted only vaguely of whisky.

"Lieutenant Ashley, sir."

As Ashley turned to face Spanier, he managed to hide the flask behind him. "At ease. What made Heydt take off in the buggy?"

Spanier started to shrug, thought better of it, then realized he had been put at ease and resumed the shrug. "Something came over the air. Some signal or other. He jumped up and yelled something about 'they're landing the stuff behind the Sunken Forest.' To tell you the truth, sir, I didn't listen too closely to him because we were monitoring another transmission. Some message from a ship at sea." Spanier shuffled sideways a bit and Ashley turned with him to keep the flask out of sight.

He had never trusted Spanier, any more than his buddy, Heydt. Of the two, he considered Spanier the sneakier. There was something at least defiant and unyielding about Chief Heydt. You knew he hated you and he knew you hated him and it was an arrangement both of you could live with. But Spanier continued to pretend he was friendly. He acted out some ritual farce of loyalty and fellow-understanding that disgusted the lieutenant. Ashley longed for the obstinate, secretive Heydt, rather than this sly toady.

"You're lying, Spanier," Ashley said coldly.

"Sir!"

"You always lie and you're lying now." Ashley smiled unpleasantly. "You weren't monitoring anything. You were listening to the broadcast band as usual, for news of Lindbergh. And finding it hard at that hour to bring in any station because they're all off the air. That's why you didn't hear whatever Chief Heydt heard."

"That's not so, sir," Spanier complained. He had worked up an aggrieved tone of martyrdom with his very first words.

"When the Chief comes back, we'll see who's right and who's lying."

Spanier's face went baldly still. "Yes, sir," he said.

Ashley had the feeling he'd made a mistake. Spanier was now giving a creditable imitation of Heydt's nasty poker face. Something Ashley had said had tipped off Spanier. "Who was the man on duty with you? Kinch?"

"Yes, sir."

"Get going. Send Kinch in here on the double."

"Yes, sir." Spanier turned to go.

"And if he's more than a minute in getting here, I'll have both of you up for company punishment on charges of collusion and insubordination. Understand?"

"Yes, sir." Spanier took a step toward the door.

"'Ten'shun!" Ashley yelped.

Spanier stiffened, turned, and froze at attention in a salute. "Permission to leave, sir."

Ashley returned the salute. "Dismissed." Spanier whirled and took off down the corridor.

Ashley had no doubt that Kinch had been coached to confirm almost any kind of story Spanier chose to tell. It now began to appear that Heydt had some other reason for leaving which Spanier was at some pains to conceal. It seemed quite possible that the night, which had left so many unexplained things in its wake, still hid a few more surprises.

Heydt should have returned long before this, unless he'd bogged down in sand or something equally foolish. He wouldn't have allowed himself to run out of gasoline, not an experienced man like the Chief. And even if he had, there was a telephone available in Cherry Grove and one in Ocean Beach from which he could have made contact with the station and asked for a small boat to be sent down the bay to bring him back, or bring gasoline for the buggy.

Ashley heard Kinch's footsteps along the corridor. He composed himself into a proper face of inquisition. He really already knew what he had to know.

Or, rather, that he had to get out and learn more. Quickly, he rejected the inquisition. He nodded curtly as Kinch saluted. "Round up my launch crew. Tell them to check their ammo and be at the launch in five minutes with rifles. Then you go directly to the launch and refuel her. Top up all tanks."

"But, sir?"

"Yes?"

"I understood you'd sent them all—that is, all of us—off duty, sir."

Ashley nodded again. "Quite right, Kinch. I told them

203

they could get some sleep. Now I'm telling them they can't. It's simple. The commanding officer commands. Dismissed."

Kinch saluted and left. Ashley made his way along the corridor to where the charts were kept and pulled one off the wall rack. He studied the familiar shoal waters along the bay side of Fire Island west of Point O' Woods, past Cherry Grove and much farther east at Long Cove. Although the shore was fairly free of hidden bays and coves, the bay was at low tide. The shallows were such that if he spotted anything to investigate, in many cases he'd have to beach the double-ended launch on her side in shoal waters and wade ashore.

He had no clear idea of what he was looking for, other than Harry Regan. The peculiar suspiciousness of Spanier, of Heydt's departure and his failure to return, made Ashley wonder if he weren't missing something more.

Perhaps contraband had been landed. Perhaps it was being transshipped over the barrier beach and across the bay to the mainland of Long Island. The whole battle at the freighter had been peculiar anyway. Perhaps it had been a feint to lure him away.

He wondered if he had enough time, while his men were readying themselves for the new patrol, to sneak off to the dune behind which he'd buried what remained of that case of whisky. He needed only a few minutes to replenish his flask.

Chapter 31

Outwardly, Harry decided, he had tidied up nicely. He'd managed to rig a triangle of sail on the stubby mast and, gaining way, had set the *Deirdre* on a northwest course that would, depending on how far he'd floated while unconscious, run him ashore on Fire Island Beach, Long Island, or the Connecticut shore of Long Island Sound.

He'd also been able to swab the hole in his breast with iodoform and place an ochre-colored court plaster six inches square over the whole area, like an immense patch on an inner tube.

He'd done it all without help from Timmy because somewhere along the way he'd lost the old man. Was it in the fight? Was it when the corvette tried to ram him? Or was it later as the *Deirdre* exhausted her supply of gasoline in blind flight?

Harry sat on the stern thwart of the boat in a bent-over position, reducing himself in size as if hiding from a great injury. He had stopped trying to feel his chest. Despite occasional sips of whisky he felt completely chilled. He had draped part of a sail over him, but it did little to quell the shivering inside him.

He wondered if Timmy had been alive or dead when he'd gone overboard. Not that it made much difference in this sea. May was none too soon for the sharks to begin cruising offshore waters. They usually started north along the coast in April.

He tried to imagine Timmy dead. They'd been through an awful lot, including near-death. But it hadn't been a miss this time. It was no good to become attached to anybody. They all had to be treated with the same casual interest you paid a woman. That was it. Interest, but not attachment. But what did you do with a dodo like Timmy, who attached himself to you?

He should have turned Timmy loose long ago. It wasn't right, letting a goofy old man like that—sixty-five if he was a day—feed his little habit like a dope fiend. Timmy had been addicted to excitement. At an age when the old soldiers' home should have claimed him, he was still chasing adventure.

And nothing tame for old Timmy. The real thing with real bullets, or he wasn't interested.

Harry told himself now that he was going to turn loose all the people he knew. If he ever got out of this alive, he would send Maeve back to her family, randy pack of scamps they were, too. He would shun the Widow Purvis.

He would give Goldie to Paul Lachaise, as if they needed the invitation. He would swear off all of them and go find himself a city job, something impersonal, work for the government or a bank, lose himself in a crush of millions of people, none of whom cared if he lived or died. And he would care even less for them.

Perfect. It was the only way to die. Live, that is.

He realized abruptly that his mind was wandering. He concentrated very earnestly on the compass in his hand. The moon had gone down long ago, but there was a very faint lightness in the east that gave him enough illumination to read the swinging compass card as it wheeled and bobbed in its vessel of oil.

Turn the whole pack of them loose, the whole race of them. Everyone ought to get himself hermetically sealed. One of those giant mason jars with the red rubber gasket and the wire clamp. Lives should be lived in isolation, like herrings pickled in brine.

Lindbergh had the right idea. Get up and get out. Live or die. Get to Paris or drown in the drink. The hell with anybody or anything.

From now on, Harry told himself, he was going to shut himself off from people. Only people had the power to make you feel bad. They died and you felt the loss. Even a low-down, toothless, nobody drunk like Timmy. Why in hell should his death make anybody feel bad?

He started to pitch forward and caught himself just in time. He hunched back on the thwart for a more secure position. He knew he was dizzy now and he figured that although the outside hole had been plugged and patched, there had to be internal bleeding. Dewar's was a fine drink, but it wasn't the absolutely proper replacement fluid for blood.

He laughed and coughed. The motion of his chest sent an immense jolt through his upper trunk as if he had been transfixed by a dull spear.

He sat absolutely still and tried to quell the tickle at the back of his throat. It was important. It was not important. Nothing had meaning. Lachaise was right. "Unreal we are all," he had said. Sounded like an Irishman, he did.

"Everything's changing, Harry Regan."

Harry nodded in agreement. He could hear Paul's full, sodden voice, with its sonorous vowels and cut-glass consonants.

"The whole world's changing. And when the changing is over, none of anything will be real."

"Damned, damned right," Harry said aloud. He felt the wind shove the words back onto his tongue. He started to cough and then suppressed it. The cough had no meaning other than his life or death. Life had no meaning, nor had death. Meaning had no meaning. Right, Harry told himself.

He wondered woozily what the new meaningless world would be like. He already knew the killing would go on. It had to spread. Never mind your League of Nations and your disarmament pacts. It was in the nature of the human animal to kill for the thrill of it. Kill first, find excuses later.

The killing would engulf so many people that killing, too, would have no meaning. First they'd be killed in all the good old-fashioned ways: starvation, overwork, poor living conditions, ignorance. Then they'd be killed in a lot of new ways nobody understood yet. But they'd find the ways. Just as they'd found them in the War. Bullets and shells and torpedoes and bombs were only the beginning. Tanks and aeroplanes and dirigibles and submarines were only the beginning.

One day, in the new world, they would be able to wipe out whole armies and navies. But they wouldn't stop at that. Behind the lines there would still be children who could grow up to fight and women who could bear new children and old-timers who could make the weapons. So they would wipe out their civilians, too. Bloodlust is a stern master.

It was dark around him. He could have sworn there had been light in the east, but there was only night now. He grinned and opened his eyes and was only mildly pleased to see that there was, indeed, light in the east.

Planes would follow Lindbergh, carrying bombs. That much was very clear.

Harry closed his eyes again. It was too bad, really, to come back to land. It was better out here. You were alone and you could make a good death for yourself out here, you and the *Deirdre* and the hell with anybody else.

He lay down on the thwart and tried to pull the bit of sail over his chest. The tickle in his throat bothered him but some stubborn streak kept him from coughing and tearing his insides further apart.

Stubborn streak of masochism, Harry thought. Only a masochist could face the new world. You had to reduce your senses to nothing and stop feeling. Otherwise you could never survive in such a world.

De-sen-si-tize. It was like those old collodion-plate photographs.

He could remember as a boy thirty years ago in the Park Slope section of Brooklyn when the photographer came around with his shaggy, matted pony and his black rubberized tarp. He would set up the tarp as a kind of tent over his tripod and camera and stir in a narrow, high, square tank his mixture of collodion and silver salts. Then he would coat a glass plate with the mixture and clap the glass inside a wooden plateholder.

Your father would put you on the patient little pony and get you steady. Your older sister, Mary, would stand beside you with young Paddy, the three-year-old, in her arms. None of the others kids had been born yet, Harry recalled very clearly.

Using the tarp now as a focusing cloth, the photographer would get your picture all set—three kids and a pony for the price of one picture—and slip the plateholder onto the back of the camera. He'd withdraw the black slide while holding a cap over the lens. You had to smile and smile and keep on smiling. He'd remove the cap for a moment, replace it, shove the safety slide back in the plateholder, and take it from the camera.

You got your maroon-sepia print a few days later. Paddy had been frowning like an ape, but your parents thought the photograph was grand.

Harry understood that now he had set his face into the rictus of that fixed smile of thirty years ago. He tried to relax his mouth and cheeks.

The photographer had sensitized the plate. It was alive to your face, your smile, Paddy's frown, Mary's dark beauty.

In the new world to come, you had to de-sen-si-tize yourself.

The old collodion photographer never came back after that year. The ones that came around later had the Kodak film plates same as you could buy for your Hawkeye or Brownie. The film was already sensitized. But if it wasn't used right away, or light got at it by accident, it was de-sen-si-tized.

Harry knew he had to do that to himself in the new world to come, or he would die. On the whole, he thought now, perhaps it was better just to forget the whole thing, strike the little rag on the mast, and let the sea swamp the poor dear *Deirdre* of the Sorrows and send her to the bottom.

And you with her. Just the two of yez.

God, the beauty of such a death. Such beauty wasn't to be allowed in the gritty, frayed-nerves world to come.

Harry shifted unhappily beneath his shelter of canvas.

He could feel the *Deirdre* spinning around slowly, like an ungainly, lopsided top, with him in the center.

The vertigo made him grab at the thwart for steadiness. Then he passed out again.

Chapter 32

"When whippoorwills call," Goldie sang softly to herself, "and evening is night, I—"

" 'Nigh,' " Lachaise interrupted. "Not 'night.' Rhymes with 'my.' "

He was standing at the living-room window, staring out at the sea. From some half-forgotten hiding place of Goldie's he had resurrected an antique telescope she had once bought at an auction. It was an amazing instrument, heavy, with three brass tubes bound by riveted copper bands. Its eyepiece was carved ebony. Lachaise had found a way of lowering one of the window sashes and resting the front end of the telescope on the ledge while holding the other end to his eye. He swiveled from side to side, causing the telescope to swing through a small arc of surveillance.

" 'Nigh'?" Goldie asked. "What the hell kind of word is 'nigh'?"

"Plain, ordinary English." Lachaise gave up his vigil after a moment and set the telescope down on the window sill. "Goddamned thing weighs a ton."

"Does it work?"

"Of course it works."

"I meant, you don't plug it in or anything?"

"I said it worked," Lachaise repeated. "Here. Try it."

Goldie shook her head. There were thick brownish circles under her eyes from lack of sleep. In the pale dawn light, Lachaise noticed, she looked a good ten years older than she really was. He frowned. "Go to bed."

She shook her head again. "Too nervous to sleep."

"He's okay," Lachaise assured her.

"You know that."

He nodded vehemently. "I'm sure of it."

"You're full of shit, Paul. But I love you. He's dead somewhere is what."

"Wrong."

"I'm sure of it," she mimicked him. "It's a feeling I've had all night."

"Just melancholy. Nothing else."

". . . cuddle up and don't be blue," Goldie sang. "All your fears are foolish fancies, maybe." She scratched her head slowly, thoughtfully. "I don't get these feelings often," she said. "Remember what I told you about the World Series?"

Lachaise gave her a pained look. "A lot of people thought the series was fixed that year."

"Those are the same chumps who think it's fixed every

year," Goldie said. "But when I get a feeling, it's a real feeling. I'm psychic, honey. You know that. And I tell you that gonif's dead."

Paul turned his back on her and picked up the telescope. He propped it on the window ledge and resumed his search of the ocean. "Funny," he said then. "Not even one of those fishing trawlers. Just those two Coast Guard boats an hour ago, on their way home, I guess."

Goldie yawned and switched on the radio. She waited for the tubes to glow and began switching the tuning lever from side to side too quickly to bring in any station clearly. Static rattled in the earphones. Lachaise put down the telescope and took over the tuning of the radio. "Too early for any station to be on," he said.

"They ought to stay open all night so we can know what's happened to Lindy."

"You're sweet," Paul told her. "Your inamorato is missing, maybe the victim of foul play, and all you can worry about is a man you never even met. A man you haven't thought about once all night."

"Lay off, Paul." She turned away from him with a petulant shrug. "I need to have my mind taken off things. Find out what Lindy's doing."

Lachaise tuned more and more slowly on the trail of a vagrant sound that hadn't seemed to be static when he'd turned past it before. After a moment he was able to zero in on it, a faint, hoarse imitation of a voice, as if produced by a trick dog.

"Harnsch, harnsch," the voice said. "Ah-harnsch."

"He's landed in Paris," Lachaise announced.

"Go to hell."

Someone began to pound loudly on the side door near the walk. Goldie's eyes rounded. "Go see, Paul, huh?"

Lachaise switched off the radio to save the batteries. He made his way to the side door and opened it to stare into the narrow gray-skinned face of Lt. Ashley, whom he had never met before. The man's yellow hair peeped out beneath one side of his cap.

"Yes?"

"The residence of Goldie Fain?"

Paul turned back slightly and shouted to the rear. "Goldie, got a dime? It's Western Union."

Ashley shoved past him and walked inside the house. He turned in the direction of Goldie's answering voice and confronted her in the living room.

"Lieutenant Ashley, United States Coast Guard," he said in a flat voice. "Miss Fain, you may be in a lot of trouble."

Nervously, Goldie tried to ruffle her hair into a semblance of order. "What trouble, Lieutenant?"

"You are an acquaintance of a certain Henry G. Regan, a known smuggler and dealer in contraband."

"I am?"

Paul came up behind Ashley. "You're indoors, Lieutenant," he said. "Didn't the Coast Guard ever teach you to take off your hat?"

He could see the color rise above Ashley's tight collar. Quickly, Ashley doffed his hat. Lachaise watched the straight blonde hair, parted in the middle, flop dankly as the Coast Guard officer turned on him. "Your name?"

Paul sketched a faint who-knows gesture. "What gives you the right to break in here, Lieutenant, and start bellowing all kinds of stupid questions?"

"I don't think it's stupid to want to know who I'm talking to."

"To whom I'm talking," Lachaise corrected with a slight baring of the teeth. "How can you expect to make Captain if you don't watch your language, Lieutenant?"

Ashley's face suddenly contorted, as if he'd sustained a delayed blow somewhere inside him. Then, quickly: "You one of Regan's gorillas, left to guard her?"

Lachaise gave him a wounded look. "My dear man," he said. Then he gave up the struggle and turned to Goldie. "Tell him, darling."

"He's Paul Lachaise," she said in a tired voice. "He's an actor."

"An actor?" Lachaise reproved. "The actor. Lachaise, *the* actor."

He watched a curious play of expressions on Ashley's face that seemed to have nothing to do with what was being said. They were in response to something else, almost as if he'd been kicked in the stomach or something equally violent.

"You all right, Lieutenant?"

"That's my business." Ashley turned back to Goldie. "Regan's my business, too. You people are known to be friendly with him. He's been observed on these premises several times over the past few months. That makes you a prime suspect, Miss Fain."

"In what?" she asked.

"That's my business."

"That's the second time you've said that," Lachaise observed helpfully.

The Coast Guard officer seemed to be in some kind of trouble, Lachaise realized. He seemed to be struggling to master himself and get himself straightened away on a more secure basis. "That's Coast Guard business," Ashley said at last. He looked a bit easier as he said it. "Coast Guard business," he repeated unnecessarily, "and it's going to stay that way."

"Good," Paul said. "Is that all?"

"Not by a long shot. I'll be back later."

"With a search warrant?" Paul asked.

"I told you this was Coast Guard business."

"I've heard it said," Paul assured him. "But neither Miss Fain nor I are swabbies in your company whom you can push around. To us you're just a Boy Scout with a boat. And if you want to rummage around in the home of a private citizen you'd better damned well have the proper legal papers or you'll get sued for everything my lawyers can dream of."

Ashley took a long, steadying breath. Lachaise watched him try to calm himself again and this time he seemed to do it more easily. Lachaise sniffed.

"Good Christ, Goldie," he said then, grinning maliciously, "this maniac's stewed to the gills. Did you ever hear that one before?"

"You're kidding."

"Do I ever kid?" Paul asked rhetorically. They had slipped into a kind of vaudeville patter, formalized and timed differently from normal conversation. "If I tell you a man in the uniform of the United States Coast Guard is making his rounds on official business dead drunk, then you'd jolly well better believe a man in the uniform of the United States Coast—"

"That's enough," Ashley managed to say. "I'll be back."

"Sober?"

"The hell with you, mister."

"Drunk and obscene," Lachaise noted. "And in the presence of a lady."

"That?" Ashley asked. His flat blue eyes flicked past Goldie's face. "That's what we call 'legger's gash,' mister." He smiled thinly at Paul. "Does it ever bother you that you're second best in there?"

Paul's right fist shot past Ashley's chin without landing. As he tried to recover his balance and throw another punch, Ashley showed him the small round eye in the muzzle of his .45 Colt automatic. "I'll be back," he said, and left the house.

Paul locked the side door, then made a circuit of the house, locking the back door and the door to the front deck. By that time he'd regained his composure and was breathing rather calmly. He found Goldie collapsed in a puddle of white crepe de chine, sobbing softly into a handkerchief. He sat down beside her on the wicker sofa and put his arm around her.

"Easy," he said. "We know Regan's alive now, don't we?"

"Wh-who cares?" she sobbed. "Did you hear what he called me?"

"Rather unusual way of putting it."

She turned her face up to him. "It was nice of you to take a crack at him, honey." She sniffed. "You didn't have to do that."

"It seemed called for. And it got him offstage."

Goldie suddenly roused herself. "We've got to get off the island, Paul." She stood up and began pacing the room. "There's no ferry till this afternoon, but plenty of guys with boats are willing to taxi you across if you make a deal with them."

"Now? It's hardly light yet."

"Why don't you slip into town and see if anybody's stirring along the docks. We can be out of here in half an hour, long before that ape comes back."

"He's not coming back. That's just talk."

Goldie shook her head. "He'll be back. I know it."

"The way you knew Regan was dead?"

"We don't know he isn't. We only know the Coast Guard thinks he isn't." She made shooing gestures. "Get going, will you, honey? I want to be off the island before he gets back."

"Or before Regan comes here." Paul gave her a disgusted look. "I'm surprised at you, letting the Coast Guard rattle you."

"It isn't that."

"Sure it is. You don't want to be here if Regan needs help."

She started to deny it again, then stopped. "How come you understand me that well, Paul?"

"That's my business," he said, imitating Ashley's flat voice.

"I guess I'm going yellow, or something."

Lachaise nodded slowly. "Shit-green. You're willing to leave him in the lurch. Just walk out on him. Just to save your own skin. It isn't hard to know what you're up to. It sticks out a mile."

Her mouth framed a series of replies, then went slack. "All right. Have it your way. But what makes you think he needs me? All of a sudden you're a big Regan expert?"

Lachaise began searching among the pillows on the white wicker sofa. "It doesn't take anything to know he's in trouble. And the poor chump is under the impression you're his girl."

"What you don't know about Regan. He's got girls salted away from one end of this island to the other." Goldie squinted at him. "What're you rooting around in that for?"

"I had an ascot last night. It's around here somewhere."

"What the hell do you need an ascot for?"

"I'm going down to the bay and see about a boat."

She smiled. "Thank God you're listening to reason. Soon as you find the boat, we'll—"

"Soon as I find one, I'm going to have it hidden away somewhere. I think if Regan comes here for help, the first thing he'll need is a getaway boat."

Goldie's face went red. "What is this with you, Paul? What's suddenly got you, playing pratboy for Harry Regan?"

"Just a sense of fitness of things."

"What's that supposed to mean?"

He found a blue-and-red paisley ascot crumpled down under a cushion, pulled it out, and tried to smooth away the wrinkles in the silk. "Just that he means something to me. Obviously he doesn't mean as much to you as your own skin."

"You going for boys these days?"

Lachaise knotted the ascot at his throat and tucked the ends inside his knitted white tennis shirt. "Listen, you idiot bitch. You and I are so used to thinking of nothing but ourselves that maybe you'll never understand what I'm saying. Maybe I won't even be able to explain it. But that man stands for something I don't want to see run down."

"Booze," Goldie snapped.

"Not funny."

"He stands for booze and so do you. Supply and demand."

"I thought you were the kid with the serious ideas," Lachaise said. "Or was that just a lot of applesauce?"

Goldie flapped a hand in disgust, the fingers arching backward disdainfully. "Don't give me that apcray, Paul. I know the lines. Harry's a free soul. He's pure because he's free. And if you tie down his freedom, it's like caging a wild bird. I saw the play, honey. What was it, Chekhov? Ibsen?"

Lachaise glanced in the mirror over the fumed-oak sideboard. He adjusted the tightness of the ascot. "I guess it's no fun for you, going through life with a permanently kinked brain," he said. "But you're no different from any other player." He turned to her. "Okay, I admit it. Regan appeals to my sense of drama. There's something theatrical about the man, sure. But it goes deeper. Did you ever wonder why you go for him? He's a crook, isn't he? Why do you go for a crook? What about the what'shisname character you were romancing two years ago, the gambler? What is there about crooks that gets under your lovely skin, Goldie?"

She shrugged and began scratching the back of her head again. "Don't make with the riddles, Paul. Get us a boat instead."

"Because players are crooks, too. My God, Goldie, the trouble with you is you don't know your history. It hasn't been more than a hundred years since players were considered the lowest of scum, clowns, rascals, thieves."

"Speak for yourself, honey."

He smiled in spite of himself. "Never mind about me, sweetheart. Thieves like you and me and Harry Regan at least have one form of life to look down on." He started for the side door.

"Okay. What?"

"Politicians." He gave her a large stage grin and left the house, closing the door firmly behind him.

Chapter 33

A fit of shivering brought him around. Harry Regan tried to sit up and found that he had gotten tangled in the piece of sail wrapped around him, almost like a sleeper in a nightmare, strangling in his sheets.

He fought for a moment with the shroudlike covering. The movement seemed to stir his blood a little. He sat up on the stern thwart of the *Deirdre* and immediately saw the pillar of smoke on the horizon.

He could not yet make out the shoreline. Nor could he tell, of course, what shoreline it might be. But the pillar of smoke rose almost vertically, with a slight drift to one side. Harry glanced at the compass and saw that the wind had shifted once again. In the dim gray light of early dawn, the wind had veered back from the east and was blowing both the smoke and the *Deirdre* toward the west.

Harry scratched about in the open case of whisky and

found a bottle with its neck smashed open. He cautiously lifted the jagged glass to his lips and poured a quantity of Scotch down his throat. He felt warmer for a moment and, eventually, a little better.

He could see the flat sandy beach now. It rose straight before him, and the sound of the surf could also be heard. It was Fire Island Beach. There was no mistaking the gradual upsweep of the sand from the edge of the combers, as they broke in long rolling trains, up a hundred yards or so to the high, grass-crowned dunes.

It was from just back of the dunes that the pillar of smoke arose. Harry half stood as he peered at a slight notch in the dune's green-flecked ridge. He knew that notch. The *Deirdre* and the wind had brought him back to Long Cove, to his own cabin.

The sound of the surf was louder now. Harry tried to think. During the night, at some point, there had been fires along the beach, two of them. It was always possible, of course, that he was mistaken. The wavy crest of the dune had many notches. His eyes were by no means in great shape.

But nevertheless, by God, it might have been his own shack that had burned. It might be the ruins of it that now sent a pillar of smoke into the sky like a beacon, welcoming home the *Deirdre* and him.

Then what of Maeve?

Harry let the sail drop from his shoulders. He moved cautiously forward into the cuddy cabin and picked up the Luger Parabellum and its snail magazine. As the momentum of the onrushing waves built higher, the wind drove the *Deirdre* faster toward the shore.

He holstered the Parabellum and tucked the magazine into his belt. Then he crept forward along the narrow bit of deck that led past the cuddy to the bow of the *Deirdre*. In a few moments she would waddle into the surf and he wanted to be able to jump free. If he had any strength left in him at all, he wanted to be able to get through the surf and up the beach to where the pillar of smoke rose, like the whitish plume of a cavalier's hat.

The *Deirdre* was only a dozen yards from shore now. Harry felt her bow rise suddenly in the grip of one of the big waves, the kind that came once in every eight or nine. Her long sprit dug down into the water. The angle of the boat shifted awkwardly and Harry was unable to grasp for support in time.

He slide off the foredeck into the icy water. The chilling shock sent a wave of raw energy through him. Ahead he could see the giant wave curve, drop, and burst into roaring whiteness. The following wave was small and calm.

Harry's legs worked faster than he thought possible. He moved jerkily through the undertow of the gentle wave and reached the shining strand. His wet boots crunched through pebbles and kicked aside cottony puffs of spume. He was on dry land.

He turned for a moment. The *Deirdre* seemed stranded where he had left her. Something in her own bouyancy was preventing the waves from carrying her into the certain wreckage of the surf. She wallowed sideways again.

Harry turned away. He didn't want to see her swamp and die. Running, falling, half-crawling, he made his way up the dune and over the notch to the pillar of smoke.

He dropped down the back of the dune, skidding on his buttocks and heels through the loose-packed sand. Abruptly he came to rest. He was looking at the charred remains of his cabin.

There was no mistaking it. The radio antenna wire ran at a crazy angle from its post to the ruins. Nearby stood the Coast Guard's beach buggy. Harry squinted through the grayish light. There were bodies.

He crawled through the sand to where the front of the house had collapsed. Something big and blackish lay in a tangle where the door had been. He recognized the Chief Petty Officer's insignia on Heydt's sleeve and wondered how it had been spared from burning.

He braced his feet against Heydt's body and rolled him sideways.

Maeve's lovely, soft black hair was burned away in patches. She had died face down with Heydt's body arched over her, not quite touching her back. Ellen had died without a mark on her.

He got to his feet and stared down at the bodies. The pain in his chest ebbed and flowed like the rise and fall of embers glowing in the heart of a furnace. He knew what had killed Heydt. The gun in Maeve's hand made that clear enough. But what had killed her and Ellen without marking them?

He decided that the fire had stolen the breath from them. They had died of suffocation, most likely. He tried to piece it all together, putting everything in a sequence. Heydt had brought Ellen here, that was obvious. And then—

He stopped himself. He was doing his little puzzles to keep himself from feeling anything. Better to do the timetable thing than to realize that both these women had loved him and died for it.

That was it, of course. He knew it could be nothing else. Heydt had tried to get at him through the women. Harry stared hard at the yellow back of Ellen's head, wondering what had happened now to all that great load of greed and frustration there. Totally untouched. Unmarked. As if sleeping. Dead only casually, tangentially. Death by association. With him.

Maeve's young body had gotten the worst of it. Burning brands had fallen on her nightgown, scorching it. Her hair . . .

Harry felt a great sob well up inside him like a bubble of his own immortal soul, choking him until he gasped in agony.

He sank to his knees in the sand and touched Maeve's burned hair. He turned her face out of the sand so that he could look at her. She hadn't deserved any of this.

She had given and given. If there were any justice to life, Ellen might have deserved this. But not Maeve. He brushed the sand from her cheek. It was amazing how little marked she was, now that he had turned her partly over on her side.

As he watched, she coughed weakly.

Chapter 34

After he and Patsy and Aldo had tied up the corvette, Maxie had transferred what guns and ammo he had left to the 32-foot cruiser. Instead of heading back out to the open Atlantic through the Shinnecock Inlet, as he had during the night, he turned west and started moving quickly through the channels that led behind the barrier beach past Quogue and Westhampton until he reached the wider stretches of Moriches Bay.

He knew that if Regan ran true to form, he or his men would try to salvage what they could of the operation by running the booze over the dunes to the bay. And, while the Coast Guard might be combing the Atlantic side of the beach, Maxie would be running west along the bay side.

He cleared the narrows at Smith Point and sent the powerful cruiser rushing headlong into the broadening expanse of Great South Bay. Maxie had been unable to raise either Heydt or Spanier on the radio and he had to find out for himself whether the Chief had effectively taken care of the two escape relays Regan could count on, his own cabin and Purvis's.

Neither Aldo nor Patsy had spoken since the last of the bodies had gone overboard. Maxie had the feeling that the prevailing ocean current would fetch most of the bodies up at the far western tip of Fire Island within a day or two, piling them up at the jetty off Democrat Point only a few miles from the Coast Guard station. They would give the swabbies and the local johns something to chase their tails around with for a while.

Maxie tried to think with the mind of Harry Regan. He knew very little about the man. He didn't even know for certain if he were still alive. But something about the way Regan had handled himself in the hijack attempt told Maxie the bastard was alive somewhere and up to no good.

If so, Maxie wanted to bring his head back to Brooklyn in a hatbox. If he couldn't show anything else for this night, he had to show his principals that Regan would never again flout their control of the beach. Nor would any other free lance, if Regan had gone down to defeat.

He steered the cruiser past Old Inlet Bay and Ridge Island. He didn't know this section of the bay beach that well, but his chart showed him that the next big hook of land dipping out into the bay signaled Long Cove harbor.

"Aldo?" Maxie waited until the man appeared at his elbow. "Guns all ready?"

"Sure, Maxie."

"Got enough ammo?"

"You bet."

"Remember. The first guy who plugs that redheaded bastard gets an extra C-note. But I gotta have the body. Capeesh?"

"*Si. Senza dubbio.*"

"Atsa my boy," Maxie said in his mock Italian accent. "Pass the word to Patsy, goombar."

"*Si. Bene.*" Aldo left with the message. Maxie thought for a while about the wonderful disciplinary power of death.

There was nothing quite like it. You could talk yourself blue in the face, but the only thing that really kept the boys in line was showing them a few dead ones.

Maybe, Maxie thought, it might have been possible to dump just the farmers. Maybe he could have spared the wounded among his own troops. But not really. What good would it have done? Aldo and Patsy would have spent the rest of the morning patching them up and, even so, some would have died anyway.

No, he had done the right thing. No walking wounded. No nursing home. He needed Aldo and Patsy right where they were, beside him now.

Ahead, on shore, a plume of whitish smoke rose into the sky. Maxie cut the engines and swerved left toward Long Cove harbor. If he knew Heydt, the smoke was what was left of Regan's shack.

He killed the engines and drifted into shore. Aldo tied

up to a gnarled piece of driftwood buried deep in the sand. Moving silently and using hand signals he had learned in the infantry, Maxie deployed Aldo to the right, carrying a Thompson chopper, and Patsy to the left with Lacoste's old double-barreled shotgun.

Maxie moved slightly ahead, at the point of the formation, holding the Beretta in front of him, a shell chambered and ready to fire.

At first all he could see was blackened pieces of timber from which the whitish smoke rose in a single column. Then he saw beyond the charred ruins to the beach buggy.

Regan was busy tying a girl to the board seat of the buggy. Maxie raised the Beretta and took careful aim. He was a little too far for accuracy but maybe he'd be in luck. He fired twice and saw the bullets kick up sand to the left of the buggy. Damn it!

Aldo sent a burst of chopper fire at Regan, who doubled over and half-ran, half-crawled behind a slight rise in the dune. As Aldo raised the Thompson to head height and took more careful aim, Regan appeared in a sudden flash of movement and put a 9 mm. Luger slug into Aldo's stomach.

Aldo's finger tightened convulsively on the Thompson trigger and sent a harsh volley of bullets into the gray sky as he crumpled to the ground. Maxie dropped on his stomach. He gestured to Patsy to move sideways and try to get at Regan from another direction.

Maxie realized he had chosen the wrong weapons.

Nothing they carried was accurate at this distance, while in Regan's hand the long-barreled Luger had the accuracy of a carbine. Patsy made a loping run around to the right and dropped out of sight behind a hillock of sand. Then Maxie began crawling forward through dune grass, the Beretta pointed straight ahead at the point where Regan had last appeared.

Suddenly, he saw a flash of red hair two yards to the left. The Luger made a deep coughing sound and the slug tore into Maxie's right shoulder, just below the joint. He cried out in pain.

Tears flooded his eyes. He could hear the engine of the beach buggy roar into life. "Patsy!" he screamed. "Shoot, Patsy!"

Through the mist of tears he saw Regan head the buggy up over the rise of the dune and drop out of sight, rear wheels spitting sand as the buggy headed west along the beach.

Chapter 35

Lt. Ashley could make nothing of the wreckage of the Purvis cottage. It seemed to have been deliberately touched off. The smashed kerosene lamp told that part of the story. But he wasn't at all clear why Purvis had decided to burn the house, if it had, indeed, been Purvis. In any event, Kinch told him Purvis had a wife and there was no sign of her, either.

Reluctantly, Ashley ordered his men back on the launch and headed east through the shoal water of Great South Bay. He knew there would be more to the story than a leisurely reading of the evidence could reveal. But his main job now was to locate Heydt. Or, failing that, to find any remnants of the rum fleet that might lead him to Regan. Or, as a last hope, to surprise some of the rumrunners transferring contraband across the bay.

The sun was barely reddening the eastern horizon now,

but the grayish light had gone and there was a small bit of warmth to the air. Ashley rubbed his hands together vigorously. He marveled at the fact that the pain in his gut had left him alone for the last half hour. It seemed to go away when he had important things occupying his mind. Sometimes, at any rate.

After leaving the ruins of the Purvis place, the launch had touched briefly at Cherry Grove but there had been no signs of Heydt or the beach buggy. Now the boat was bearing steadily east again, past Water Island and Leja Beach. In a few minutes they would raise the harbor at—

Ashley heard the submachine gun fire, a long burst, the longest he had ever heard. In his own experience with automatic weapons, it would have been impossible to keep the muzzle down and aimed during such a burst.

He turned back to yell at the steersman. The launch picked up speed as it rounded the point of land into Long Cove harbor.

Ashley hefted the Navy issue Springfield and snapped an eight-load magazine into it. "Pull in next to that cruiser," he shouted.

Even before the launch buried its bow in the sand, Ashley had jumped off the bow with the Springfield held at port-arms. He could hear splashes as the rest of his crew followed him.

Running at a crouch, he raced up over a rise in the sand and saw a man to his right with what looked like a shotgun. "Drop it!" he yelled.

Patsy let the shotgun fall into the sand. He raised his hands over his head without being told. The Lieutenant waved two Coastguardsmen ahead to take him.

Ashley stepped through the charred ruins of the cabin, trying to make a connection in his mind between the two fires. Then he saw Heydt's body. He dropped to one knee and felt for a pulse at the base of the Chief's throat.

"It's the Purvis woman," Kinch said behind him. His voice sounded pinched.

So intent had he been on Heydt that Ashley only now saw that the Chief's body had pinned down the body of a woman. At that moment he heard moaning from the grass to the left of the ruined cabin. He raised the Springfield. "Come out. Hands up. You're covered."

He could hear Maxie whimper with pain before he saw him struggle to his feet, still holding the Beretta. "Drop the gun."

Maxie stood there unmoving for a moment, then let the pistol drop. "My shoulder," he moaned.

"You're not Regan," Ashley said accusingly.

"Regan?" Maxie laughed bitterly.

"What's happened here? Why did you shoot Chief Heydt?"

Maxie folded at the midriff and went down face first in the sand. Ashley had two of his men carry him back to the launch and wrap his shoulder tightly with heavy gauze.

As he watched them, he saw two more of his men find

a third body in the high dune grass to one side. They dragged the corpse to Ashley. The dead man's hands held the Thompson in a tenacious grip. The whiteness of the knuckles had already spread to the fingers. Ashley had the body laid under a tarpaulin in the cruiser.

"Kinch," Ashley said. "You and Drucker put the Chief and the Purvis woman aboard the cruiser, too. Bring them all back to the station." He turned to Patsy. "All right," he said. "Your friend doesn't seem to want to talk. But there's nothing wrong with you, is there?"

Patsy moistened his lips.

Ashley glanced at Maxie. "I can get anything I want out of this one," he told the seemingly unconscious man. "Or do you want to wake up and start talking?"

Maxie moaned softly and rubbed the gauze bandage. "My arm."

Ashley leaned back against the gunwale of the beached launch. The sun had risen just over the horizon now and a thin layer of cloud, all that was left of last night's scud, turned bright salmon in the distance.

The night chill was gone and Ashley knew they were going to have one of those warm, bright days in May with the air so clear you could look twelve miles across the bay to Islip and Bayshore and see the sun glinting on the windows of houses. He wished he didn't have to deal with Regan's scum. He wished he could go off by himself down the beach and look at pebbles and shells. He wished he could give himself a day off and go casting for blues or stripers. But instead he had this whimpering scum to deal with.

"I can wait," he told Maxie then.

There was a curious half smile, half grimace on Maxie's small mouth. "So can I, Lieutenant," he said.

"Is that a fact?" Ashley eyed him more closely. While the uninjured one seemed frightened, this one seemed quite calm, despite his wound. He dressed differently from the uninjured one, too. His clothes were sharper, nattier, more expensive. The other one wore what amounted to cheap work clothes and no jacket. This one had a striped business suit cut very tight at the waist and cuffs. His shoes came to points. His haircut had cost him something, too.

"You might start by telling me," Ashley said, "what brings a city lad like you to these parts?"

"I might," Maxie agreed. "I might not."

Ashley felt his anger rising. He could not, not, not afford to let rage spoil this. He had this man dead to rights. He could turn him over to the police for the murder of Heydt and he would, too. Not that he cared a damn about Heydt. If this man had killed the Chief he had done Ashley a favor. But you didn't let anybody get away with killing a Coastguardsman. Not ever.

"You don't have to talk," Ashley told him. "The evidence does it for you. The Islip cops are going to lock you up and throw away the key. When the judge hears the story you'll be on your way to the electric chair."

Maxie smiled very tentatively. "You think I killed

him?" He jerked his chin in the direction of the cruiser, where Kinch and another man were lifting Heydt's body with some difficulty onto the deck.

"You'll fry for it as nicely as anybody else. I vote for you." Ashley smiled back. His anger seemed to have relaxed its hold.

Maxie shook his head. "Not me, Lieutenant. You got my heater. It's a .32. The Chief was killed with a bigger slug."

"That's cop business," Ashley said. "I don't have to tell them which gun is yours. I might just find a .38 or .44 around here and remember it belonged to you."

Ashley waited in silence for a sign that he had shaken the man. He knew he could never do all that he was threatening. But he also knew the man had no way of knowing just how much he might try. It was a test, in a way, of what kind of fish Ashley had caught in his net.

Maxie shook his head again. "Don't scare me, Lieutenant. I cry easy."

Ashley frowned. He hadn't caught a worm. It was more like a shark. And, worst of all, it seemed to be a shark with a strong sense of belonging to a school of sharks. Ashley recognized the feeling. He was dealing with someone who didn't feel at all alone.

Maxie's grin began to get to him again. He had to keep remembering not to lose his temper. "In that case," Ashley said slowly, "you're going to shed an awful lot of tears, mister."

Maxie's grin widened easily until his small, white teeth

shone. "Have it your way, Lieutenant. But there is nothing here to tie me to anything. When my lawyers get through with you, you'll be lucky if the Coast Guard doesn't court-martial you for giving false testimony in a civil trial."

Ashley turned away to hide his face. The pain in his gut had flared up again and he didn't want this little runt to see what it did to his face. He recognized the same bluff he himself had tried. This was going to be a stand-off. But not quite. He still had the man in his hands. He might turn out to be a shark, but he was gaffed shark, beached and gasping for breath.

Ashley wondered what made the little man so bold. The other one, the one with the shotgun, had panicked. Not this one. Perhaps he should separate them and work on the uninjured one. He would yield enough information to use in breaking down the calm one.

The trouble was that Ashley didn't have the time, place, or men to try this simple tactic. Moreover, with the murder of Heydt, this had become a clear-cut police matter. Ashley was already outside his own jurisdiction, or would be the moment he reported this to the civil authorities in Islip. Worst of all, none of this seemed to be leading him to Regan.

He turned back to the wounded man. "No sense arguing about it. You and the police can go around in circles. You're cooked. But Regan isn't. He's long gone. Why do you owe him anything now? Put me onto him and I can give you a good send-off to the cops. It'll go a lot better if you cooperate. You know that."

"How many times have I heard that one?" Maxie asked rhetorically.

"It still makes sense."

Maxie looked thoughtfully at Ashley. "Matter of fact, it does."

Chapter 36

Regan drove the buggy in under the high staircase that led from the beach to the village of Cherry Grove. At this hour, nobody would yet be moving about in town except people he knew.

He killed the engine and turned to look at Maeve. To keep her safe, he had had to tie her down on the plank seat beside him. He loosened the cords. He wondered how badly off she really was.

He had stripped off his black wool sweater and pulled it on her. She filled it sparsely, giving him the uneasy idea that she was shedding an old, spent skin. The thought worried him, not because he really believed his sweater was a charred skin, but because the disorderly idea had even presented itself to him. He recognized that he had troubles of the body, too many to consider. But he did not, at this point, want to cope with troubles in his mind.

Her breathing was shallow and slight, but regular. Her face, normally a bit flushed with her own excitement or passion, looked waxy-yellow, that terrible sallowness dark-haired people had in sickness. It was beyond Regan how she had escaped death. He supposed it had something to do with the way Heydt's body had jackknifed slightly as it fell over her, leaving a narrow pocket of protection and perhaps a bit of air.

The only other thing that might have saved her, he knew, was the flimsiness of his shack. There wasn't much there to burn and not for long, either. It would have made a gaudy fire, but a quick one.

Buried beneath both of them, Ellen hadn't had a chance. Nor had Heydt, with those slugs in him. Regan's mouth looked grim. It was only a matter of time before the police and the Coast Guard sorted out the whole thing. By then, he hoped, the bodies would have decomposed enough to confuse the facts. It was possible that the presence of a third person there would be overlooked. But if in the end it came to that, the police would naturally blame him for Heydt's murder, not Maeve.

That was fine. If he ever got her across the bay to a proper doctor, and if she pulled through, he was perfectly willing for the police to want him, not her. It was a price he would be glad to pay for her life.

Harry managed to get up the stairs and slipped quietly along one of the boardwalks to the home of a friend named John Ashley. He supposed Ashley and the Coast Guard lieutenant were cousins. Ashley was a common enough name in these parts. John Ashley was a general handyman-mechanic whose boat Harry had never been able to recruit for any nighttime activity. Perhaps he could borrow it now for a daylight crossing.

He rapped softly at Ashley's back door and waited. After a moment, the man opened it a crack. "It's you," he said mournfully. "Should've known it."

"Johnnie, it's your boat I need. Maeve needs a doctor bad. Can I take her across now in your boat?"

"Nothing gets across the bay this morning." John Ashley's voice had a low, keening moan to it like the tolling of a sunken buoy bell.

"The swabbies aren't out?"

"After last night, need you ask?"

"Then, look, Johnnie. Will you take her across yourself? I'll make myself scarce. But if I knew you were taking her to a doctor, I'd feel better about it."

"Gunshot wounds?"

"Nothing of the sort. There was a fire at my shack."

John Ashley seemed to hesitate for a moment. "No," he said then. "If I'm caught with her, she's known as your girl, Harry. I can't. No."

Regan's back teeth hurt from the effort of keeping his jaw clamped shut. He wanted to reach through the narrow crack into the darkened house and pull John Ashley out by his neck. "She'll die, Johnnie. No mistake. What do you say?"

"I say no."

The "no" had a tolling sound, hollow and muffled.

Harry Regan tried to push the door open wider than the more prudent crack. "Can I leave her with you, then? Just for the hour or two it takes me to bring a doctor here?"

The door started to shut. "I said no, Harry. No."

Regan's right arm braced against the door. "Johnnie, it's her life."

The door pushed shut and Regan was horrified to see that he had no strength in his right arm to stay the movement. "Johnnie?"

There was no sound from inside the house. Regan hammered on the door again but he could hear how weak the sound was, even though he was pounding as hard as he could.

"Johnnie?"

Across the street a door opened and a man stared out at him. Regan walked back toward the beach. The effort of climbing the stairs, or arguing with John Ashley, had left him much weaker now. The wound in his breast ached. Now and then a sharp flashing pain shot outwards from it like an exploding shell. He had probably torn loose the clot by hammering on the door. To hell with the clot.

He made his way slowly down the dune stairs, saving himself. With his left hand he spun the starter crank. He let his right arm lie limp in his lap as he steered the buggy down toward the strand of the beach and continued east.

He had no idea of what to do now for Maeve. Out of season there was no doctor along the entire length of

Fire Island. And if no one would help him get her across to the mainland, she would die.

Dimly he remembered thinking—when was it—that he would have to cut loose all his ties with people. Timmy was dead. Ellen was dead. Maeve would die. He was a plague. Whatever he touched died.

But he wanted her to live. It was different with Timmy or Ellen. One had been ripe for death anyway and the other had made a life not worth living. But Maeve was too young and too pure. None of this was her own doing.

She had been nearly killed in his place, for him, and by some miracle had survived. Now he had to keep her alive.

Chapter 37

There was no one to be found along the bayside docks in the village of Ocean Beach. Lachaise moved slowly from mooring to mooring, wondering why, at an hour when so many fishermen and clammers were up and about and ready to sail, the docks were empty of people.

Like everyone else on the island, he knew there had been trouble last night off the Atlantic shore. One would have had to be deaf and blind not to know. And he supposed, too, that the occasional gap where a boat had been tied up and was now missing testified to someone who had been involved in last night's fracas.

He shivered. The knit shirt and ascot were no protection at all against the early morning chill or his own feelings. His stomach still felt a little sore and his head ached, but not with the true throb of the hangover. Lachaise sat down on a stanchion and tried to sort out matters.

He was pretty sure it had been the star shells and gun-fire at sea that had brought back Belgium and Ypres, and, with them, that peculiar nausea from which there was no escape. He rarely thought about the war. He supposed anyone who had been in it also did his best not to remember. The egregious American Legion fools who were forever bragging about what they had done and now deserved from the country they defended were obvious scoundrels of some kind, he felt certain, slackers or rear-echelon scroungers or noncombattant graduates of training camps who had gotten to France just before the Armistice and were forever expiating their guilt at the expense of everyone else.

Lachaise himself had been in England, working, when it became clear that the United States was coming into the war. He enlisted in a British unit and had never been sorry about it. Like most ex-Tommies or poilus, he took a less-than-enthusiastic view of the A.E.F.'s accomplishments in Europe. He had gotten into so many fistfights back home after the war defending this incredible view that he had finally, reluctantly, decided to keep his mouth shut on the subject.

Not that anyone discussed it any more, he thought now, staring at the smooth, unbroken surface of the bay. The whole thing was a bad, demon-ridden dream that everyone had successfully forgotten.

He glanced up as someone approached him and saw it was the skinny old man who ran the grocery store. Lachaise knew him but felt sure the man—a Mr. Morris—

had only the vaguest idea who Lachaise was . . . one of that Fain woman's fancy men.

"Where's everybody?" Lachaise asked, using a swallowed-up voice that corresponded with the local dialect, vowels rubbed out into a general schwa-sound. "Wurr's uvuhbudduh?" His ear for dialects was sharp enough still that he could generally blend into almost any milieu, at least for the purposes of a brief conversation.

Morris looked at him for a moment. Lachaise could see it bothered the old man to find the local voice pattern issuing from the mouth of a stranger. "Out," Morris said, finally.

"Asleep?"

"Some."

"Damned few on the bay."

"A-yeh."

"I'm looking to hire a boat."

"A-yeh."

"Got to get across."

"Ferry?"

"Too late. Got to go sooner."

Morris started to walk away. "Anybody stirring at this hour?" Lachaise asked.

The old man stopped for a moment. "Better not be." He cackled softly and kept on walking.

Lachaise launched a long silent curse at the old man's back, involving his own personal wishes for the particular manner in which Morris was to spend eternity. It was obvious to him that even his own masterful approximation of the local mumble didn't qualify him as a genuine local. How many locals wore ascots?

Don't forget the clean fingernails, Lachaise added to himself. You flunked on fourteen counts, old man. He stood up and continued walking west along the bay front bulkhead until he came to the slight spur of land that marked the far end of the village. He glanced around him. No one was in sight. It seemed to be something after six in the morning, perhaps six-thirty. No faces were pressed to the windows. Most panes were shuttered or blank with drawn shades.

Lachaise stepped carefully into a smallish runabout, some 20 feet long. He cast off the painter and the stern line, picked up a short paddle and silently maneuvered the boat around the point of land. Then he settled back in the bow, kneeling like an Indian canoer, and paddled the boat out of sight of the village. He ran it in under some scrubby holly bushes and tied it up.

He opened the tank of the Evinrude outboard and stuck his finger inside. The tank was full. He glanced about the small boat for the starter cord, found none. Evidently this was the owner's sole precaution against theft, taking the starter cord away with him.

Lachaise screwed the tank shut and left the boat. He walked swiftly along an old car track through the deserted wasteland west of the village and reached the ridge of ocean dune in a few minutes. He struck out east for Goldie's house.

Somewhere in the house, he hoped he would find a

length of clothesline that could be cut and knotted into a starter cord. He felt sure the boat's owner wouldn't be looking for the stolen craft. It didn't have the appearance of a working boat but of one a weekender might use.

The clear morning air seemed to be helping his headache. His only problem now was Goldie's cowardice.

Chapter 38

The Coast Guard launch swept closer to the long out-
jutting wharf at Cherry Grove. Crouched in the bow beside the useless acetylene searchlight, Lt. Ashley gave a
hand signal. The steersman reduced speed so abruptly
that the bow of the launch sank for a moment almost to
the gunwales. The boat proceeded at a slower pace,
maneuvering under the tarry piles that supported the
wharf. Ashley lifted himself up onto the dock and made
fast a line. His crew climbed up after him.

He hunkered down at the edge of the dock and watched
the dapper little man in the stylish business suit. Maxie
had been laid on the curved ribs of the launch's bottom,
between the engine hatch and the bow. He looked up at
Ashley with such assurance and confidence that the
Lieutenant almost, but not quite, stood up and walked
away.

Instead he continued staring, as if hoping to burst

through the small man's impenetrable shield. "I never saw," he said then, "a man with as little appreciation of his own trouble as you."

"I never saw anybody spend so much time reminding me," Maxie returned. He grunted with pain as he raised himself to a seated position. "Or are you busy reminding yourself, Lieutenant?"

This time Ashley did get to his feet. He'd had enough of the little man. He knew that if he allowed it, his own anger would rekindle the pain inside him and, between the wounded man and his own gut, there would be no peace. He turned to face his crew, lined up at ease, each with a Springfield at ready.

"Search the town." Kinch nodded solemnly. "You're looking for Regan. For the beach buggy. For contraband or any signs it passed through here. Look for any wounded men in hiding. Got it?"

"Sir," Kinch asked, "if we locate Regan, what are our orders?"

"Alive. I want him brought back here to me. That's your first order." Ashley paused. "Second order: if you can't take him alive, shoot to kill. Is that clear?" He paused again. "Dismissed!"

Ashley watched them walk off in loose formation through the growing light. He turned to stare down at the dapper man, who was talking in low tones to the uninjured one. It was bad policy to let them confer. But something about the way the two men were talking persuaded him not to stop the conversation.

After a while, the dapper man looked up. "Lieutenant, you're right."

"About what?"

"About Regan leaving me in the lurch. So . . ." His voice died away as he adjusted himself to a less taxing position. "So maybe I can give him to you and maybe you can stand between me and the cops. Is that a deal?"

Ashley climbed down into the launch. He sat on the bow and watched the little man for a long moment. "No deals. I'll do what I can, depending on how your story sounds."

Maxie nodded. "Fair enough," he said in a tone that made it clear to Ashley the offer was unfair. "Here's the lay of it. Regan killed the Chief. He's got some kind of Heinie automatic, a Luger 9 mm., I think, and that's the caliber of slug that did the job, not my .32."

"Start with who you are, mister."

"Me?" Maxie touched his chest with upturned palms. "I'm nobody, Lieutenant. Just a little nobody. Name's Maxie Grant. This here's Patsy Fusco. I guess you could say we're small-time losers who never even got started."

"Started in what?"

Maxie grinned with mock embarrassment. It bothered Ashley that he didn't seem to be taking any great effort to make his story convincing. "In the booze business, Lieutenant. I'm being frank with you because my record's clean. I never even got started. This was my first crack at it, last night. I heard you could make yourself a pile throwing in with Harry Regan. Patsy and me had the idea we could learn the ropes that way."

Ashley nodded. "So you bought yourselves a five thousand dollar cruiser and started at the bottom."

Maxie smiled, again with no embarrassment. "I know it looks funny. But we don't own that cruiser. I mean, we borrowed it from a friend."

"Stole it."

"Borrowed, Lieutenant," Maxie repeated, again with no great effort at sincerity. "Anyway, we never even got a sniff of the action last night. We were supposed to stay tied up at Long Cove. Regan was going to start landing booze on the beach there and we were supposed to relay the stuff across the bay to Sayville and Patchogue."

Ashley nodded again. "What went wrong?"

"Regan went wrong, is what," Maxie said. "He showed up, but not by boat. He came in your Coast Guard beach buggy with the Chief driving."

"What?"

The two men watched each other warily for a moment. Ashley had expected a fairly ordinary fake story. But the sudden wild embroidery shook him. "Tell me that part again."

"Sure, Lieutenant. The Chief was chauffeuring Regan, that much I know. They got out of the buggy and started building a signal fire. There were boats out there waiting for a sign to land."

Ashley's mind stopped rejecting the story. It had begun

to take on the battered, illogical appearance of truth. "Go on."

"You remember how the wind kept shifting last night?" Maxie nodded to reinforce his own statement. "Well, the signal fire caught against the side of Regan's shack. He and the Chief had a hell of an argument. He said the Chief was trying to do him in. He didn't need the Chief any more anyway. All he needed was his beach buggy. Your beach buggy," he added.

"The Coast Guard's beach buggy," Ashley reminded him.

"Right. So he dropped the Chief with two slugs. Christ, Lieutenant, you have no idea what a crazy man this Regan was. Is. Loony as a bedbug."

Maxie paused and moistened his lips. The day was warming up and so was he, Ashley noticed. "Go on."

"Well," Maxie shrugged and the movement fired up the pain in his shoulder. He winced and nursed the gauze. A thin stain of blood was beginning to show through the bandage now and he inspected it for a moment with more attention and interest than he had paid to the story he was telling.

"Go on."

"The ships unloaded through the gap there about one–two in the morning and went back through the inlet empty. That's how I figure it, anyway. They showed up about four on the bayside and took the stuff away."

Ashley was prepared to believe most of the story. But his own caution told him no one else would believe that a flotilla of small craft that had already traveled 25 miles from the inlet to the Atlantic side of Long Cove would then make the 50-mile journey back to Long Cove on the bay side. They would have had to refuel somewhere in the small hours of the morning and there simply was no fuel depot anywhere on the Island that could handle such a demand.

"What about fuel?"

Maxie started to shrug again, but stopped himself. "They were carrying extra drums of gas."

"The hell they were," Ashley said. But he said it to himself. No rumrunner took drums of inflammable gasoline into possible battle. Instead, he nodded reasonably to Maxie. "Go on."

"That's it, Lieutenant."

"It doesn't jell. Why did Regan leave the two of you alone?"

"He was finished with us. We were supposed to get paid off in cases of booze, but he double-crossed us there, too. He loaded all the booze and had it shipped to the mainland."

"And then left you alive to tell the whole world about it."

"Who would we talk to?" Maxie's voice grew slightly more forceful, but not much. "Would we tell the cops or the Coast Guard or the revenue agents? He was safe enough."

"All right," Ashley went on. "What about the dead man with the submachine gun? I heard him fire a burst just as we started to land. I wondered what it was when I heard it." Ashley nodded significantly, more to himself than to Maxie. "As he got shot, he convulsed. That was a dead man's finger on the trigger. Who shot him? Why?"

Maxie thought for a moment. "You're a hard man to fool, Lieutenant. Okay." He swallowed, not guiltily but with ease, as if moistening his throat. "Everything I said was true, except that Regan did try to knock the three of us off. You were right, him not wanting to leave us alive. But Aldo came from behind with the chopper and the rest you know. Regan hopped it in the beach buggy and hightailed it the hell down the beach."

"Which way?"

Maxie wet his lips. "That would be telling, wouldn't it?"

"That would be telling," Ashley agreed.

"Okay." Maxie thought for a moment. "West."

Ashley let a long silence grow between them. Then: "And the Purvis woman? Could you sort of weave her into the story?"

Maxie smiled slowly. Ashley knew they had an agreement all the more binding because neither of them had spoken of it aloud. He waited patiently.

"The Purvis broad. Lemme see." His smile widened to a grin. "Okay, how's this? She was at the shack already. Everybody knew she was Regan's woman, right? She was working the shack for the booze relay. Okay?"

Ashley nodded slowly. "The only thing it doesn't take

care of is that somebody also burned down the Purvis cottage last night."

Maxie's eyes went wide, not too much, just a suitable sign of casual surprise. "Then I guess she was with Regan and the Chief. They were transferring through two places, right? They relayed some of the shipment through the Purvis place and went on to relay the rest through Regan's shack."

"And by way of a signal, they burned down both."

Ashley stood up. He could hear the first of his patrol returning from the search mission. He had already guessed they would find nothing. He was tired of listening to a story he could have invented more convincingly for himself. He wished he had more time to patch it up properly so that he could officially endorse it. Perhaps he'd find time later, before he turned in Maxie and the bodies to the police.

"They're kind of violent people, I guess," Maxie said then. His grin was so sly that Ashley wanted to kick in his mouth. "I mean, what can you expect from a wild man like Regan?"

Ashley looked him over, trying to see him as a reliable witness. He hadn't the slightest idea how much of what he had been told was true. Too much of it failed to hang together convincingly. But any seasoned interrogator knew that the truth usually had a strong thread of illogic running through it. Maybe the story would wash, maybe not. Maybe he could fix it up in time.

In any event, one thing seemed clear. For reasons too complicated to understand clearly himself, he and Maxie were now in cahoots. There was no other word to describe what lay between them.

He didn't particularly like the idea. But he'd made deals with crooks before. Any law enforcement officer had to. Often a case couldn't possibly be solved except by collusion with criminals.

The main idea was to get Regan. Any means he used to that end were justified. Any law officer knew that. Centuries of enforcement stood solidly behind the idea. If, in the process, Maxie managed to wriggle through the net, the law still came out ahead because it had the bigger fish, Regan.

Ashley's eyes narrowed slightly as he watched Maxie. He tried to see him as a little fish. The thought nagged him, but not powerfully enough to stop him from honoring the deal.

Kinch arrived on the wharf above him. "Sir? Beach buggy tracks at the foot of the dune stairs." Ashley nodded. Maxie had at least lived up to that part of the bargain. "Get back to the telephone," he instructed Kinch. "Rouse Ensign Jorgensen and have him dispatch four land patrols of five men each, armed. They're to comb the island, starting east from the station in four separate lines, one on the ocean, one on the bay, and two down the center. I want Regan alive. But, if not, I want him dead. That clear?"

Kinch saluted, about-faced, and took off on the double

for the telephone. Ashley watched him go, then turned to Maxie. "That much of your story was true, wasn't it?"

Maxie looked aggrieved. "Why, Lieutenant, I don't tell lies."

Ashley permitted himself a very small smile. "How true," he murmured.

Chapter 39

As the beach buggy jounced through the sand, the pain in Harry Regan's breast began to grow sharper. He linked the two events in his mind, but he seemed incapable of more than making the connection. His body had begun to freeze into positions from which he could not rouse it. At the moment, he had slumped to the right to give his left arm more leverage on the steering wheel and to cushion Maeve's head from the plank seat on which it lay. Somewhere inside his brain, Harry also knew that his mind had begun to freeze position too. He was losing the ability to think his way out.

Except at the Sunken Forest, where there was a notch in the dune that led back to Purvis's cottage, there was only one other place along the length of Fire Island where Harry could drive off the beach. This was another notch where Ocean Beach began, near the water tower. Although the season had not yet begun, this was hardly the best place Harry would have chosen to drive off the beach unobserved. He had no idea what the time was. By the sun it might be anywhere around seven in the morning. At that hour he ran a good risk of being seen driving off the beach.

So he would, instead, drive off at the Sunken Forest and hole up at Purvis's cottage. That was the thing to do.

There would be food there. He might have some explaining to do to Ellen about Maeve, but the poor girl was obviously so sick that even . . .

Harry grimaced. Ellen was dead.

His mind was giving out. There would be no Ellen at the cottage near Sunken Forest. But there would be food and a bed. Jim's boat was powerful enough to get them across the bay in half an hour. There was a doctor in Islip who had befriended Harry in the past. With Jim's help, he—

Regan tramped hard on the gas pedal, pushing the buggy faster through the sand. There was no Jim. Remember that. There was no Jim's boat. There was nothing at the cottage, just a dead end without an escape route.

He could hole up there and watch Maeve die and then he could follow her. If the Coast Guard didn't find him first. One thing he had no illusions about, nor was it possible to grow forgetful of it. He knew quite well that he was still losing blood internally. He also knew he had begun to lose the use of his right arm and hand.

It wouldn't be much of a death. Better if he'd gone down at sea with the *Deirdre*.

They were all dead or dying with him. He was dragging them all down. Both Jim and Ellen. Both Timmy and the *Deirdre*. Now Maeve and himself. And they were sordid, rotten little deaths. Nothing grand about them.

The buggy jounced over a pothole and Harry felt the pain shoot up his neck into his head. It felt like a rising tide of molten lead, mortifying his flesh in its wake.

He had no idea where he was now. Had he passed the notch to the Sunken Forest? Had he passed Point O' Woods? He glanced down at the speedometer and saw that he had pushed the ungainly buggy up to 20 miles per hour along the slick, wet strand.

He doubted she could go any faster. He hoped she had enough gas. He hoped he would see some sign soon of where he was and get some idea of what he was going to do.

Chapter 40

"Let's get going," Goldie whined.

She had thrown a long white silk scarf over her shoulders. It trailed down the front and back of her white lounging pajamas in Isadora Duncan style as she paced the front windows of her living room.

"Plenty of time," Lachaise assured her. "I want to wait awhile."

"That Coast Guard bastard will be back here."

"Maybe."

"I don't want to stand around being insulted any more." She glared at him. "Or maybe you get a kick out of hearing it."

"Maybe he's got your number better than I have."

"You lousy prick."

Lachaise nodded solemnly. "I thought you were somebody big. Now you want to powder out of here like a common tart in a police raid. Just sneak out the back window. Anything to keep from taking a ride in the paddy wagon."

"Right!" Goldie snapped. "Right, right, right. That's me. I want to be miles away from here when the paddy wagon rolls up. You, my fine drunken gentleman, you can stand around here all day waiting for Harry Regan if you want to. Me, I wanna powder the hell out the back window, cop a sneak, and wash my hands of the whole fucking thing. Understand?"

"You're yellow."

"Right, I'm yellow. I'm a girl. Girls don't have to be brave. I'm yellow and I'm leaving. So let's move."

Paul Lachaise laughed at her. She couldn't get serious without being funny. There was something about the way her mind worked that inevitably made him laugh at her no matter how irritating she became.

"I'm the one who knows where the boat is hidden," he reminded her. He held up a length of clothesline he had made into a starter cord. "You don't cop any sneak without me, honeybunch."

"It's not bad enough they want to question me because of Harry Regan. Now you have to go steal a boat."

He burst out laughing again. "How else did you expect us to get off this island?"

"Did you ever hear of hiring a boat?"

"I tried. Everybody's staying off the bay. They don't think it's safe out there because of what happened last night."

Goldie dug her fingers into her yellow hair. "My God, I'm going crazy!" She paced the length of the living room again. "You want me to risk my ass out there in a stolen boat when nobody else is willing to?"

Lachaise dissolved in laughter. His eyes grew moist. "Y-you're incredible," he said after a moment. "Do you want to get off this island or not?"

She stopped pacing and glanced at her tiny wrist-watch. "Seven-fifteen a.m. Time for a drink."

Lachaise rolled sideways on the sofa and buried his face in the pillow.

"What's so funny about a broad having a drink at seven-fifteen in the morning?" Goldie asked. "You of all people ought to understand."

Lachaise wiped his eyes and got up. He put together two whiskies and water and handed one to Goldie. "Your very good health," he said, "and confusion to the enemy."

Goldie stared at him for a moment, then nodded and took a swallow that drained half the drink. She gasped for breath. Then she sat down and patted the sofa beside her. "What're we gonna do, Paul?"

He sat down and looked into his drink. "Wait awhile."

"I'm afraid."

"Nothing to be afraid of."

"There's all kinds of things."

He shook his head. "The worst thing you can do is betray yourself. If you want to worry, worry about that."

"Huh?"

"You're somebody, baby. You're not a Dumb Dora

chorine or idiot flapper. You're a person. You make commitments. You have one to Harry Regan and you have one to me."

"Shit I do."

He patted her knee and ran the palm of his hand over the smooth crepe de chine. "Grow up. Maybe he's dead. It doesn't matter. I have a commitment to him and you have one to me."

"I didn't hear anybody making any deals."

He smiled and shook his head again. "Just try to get out of it. It betrays who you are. That's the worse thing you can ever do."

Goldie finished the rest of her drink and put the glass away. "My God, I must be out of my mind sitting here gassing with a rumdum actor." She grinned sideways at Lachaise. "Who the hell are you to lecture to me? Just because you do the Bard and I do Ziegfeld?"

He put his arm around her. "No. Because we always trust each other and you're going to trust me one more time. Is that a better answer?"

She considered this for a moment. Then she took his glass and sipped from it. "Tell me, why are you so hot for helping Harry Regan? You only met him last night."

"That's right. He's unusual. He's different. There's something about him I think is worth taking some trouble for."

"Damned if I get you, Paul. He's a hoodlum. A nothing."

"He didn't like my Hamlet in London."

"Right. See? So let's go."

"It was a rotten Hamlet."

She took another sip of his drink. "Kiss me."

"You're getting sleepy."

"I'm getting sexy."

He pulled away the V-opening of her pajama top to expose her bare left breast. "I can't remember, is that the one that's bigger than the other?" He began to nibble at it.

"Take off my clothes and find out."

He pulled the pajama top free of the belt and started to lift it over her head. She tensed and sat upright. "Sh!"

"What?"

"That noise."

"I didn't hear any n—"

"Sh!" She batted his hands away from her and jumped to her feet. Her immense eyes seemed to swallow up the room as they sought information. "There! Hear it?"

Lachaise stood up and moved quietly to the hallway that led back into the rear of the house. The morning sun was slanting almost horizontally through the living room and his eyes could not at first accommodate to the darkness along the hall. He stepped into the darkness. Far ahead he heard a board creak. He felt the hairs prickle along the back of his shoulders. He took another step. There was something there at the far end. If only his eyes could . . .

"Help me," Harry Regan said.

Lachaise moved quickly along the dark hallway until

271

he could see Harry standing there. He looked strangely lopsided and then Lachaise made out the girl he was holding on his left arm.

Lachaise took the girl from him and carried her into the living room. In the strong shafts of morning sunlight the burned patches on her head looked like immense scabs. Her face was impassive, eyes shut, skin the color of death. Paul put his ear to the coarse knit wool sweater she was wearing. The black wool was matted with blood. He tried to listen for a heartbeat, got none.

"Good Christ," Goldie said. "Who's she?"

Lachaise pulled off the sweater and threw it on the floor. Her nightgown looked scorched in places. He pressed his ear to her left breast and, after a moment, got a faint rustling flutter of sound. He picked up the girl and stretched her out on the wicker sofa.

"She'll bleed all over it," Goldie said.

"She's not shot. That's Harry's sweater. He's shot."

Goldie dashed into the hallway. After a moment the two of them came into the room, Goldie supporting Regan under his left shoulder. His shirt and jeans were caked with blackish dried blood. She sat him down on a chair and ripped open the front of the shirt. Paul and she examined the court plaster.

"Better leave it," Harry croaked. His voice had a dry, whispering quality about it. "Got to get her to the mainland. Doctor name of Powers. Dr. Powers. Islip." He started to fall out of the chair.

Paul eased him onto the floor on his left side. "How'd you get here, Harry?"

"Beach buggy. Don' worry. Hid it." His lids started to close as his eyeballs turned up. He passed out.

Goldie got to her feet and surveyed the living room. "Now," she said. "Now is exactly the right time for that Coast Guard bastard to show." She turned to Maeve. "Who is this little snip anyway?"

"You know as much as I do. I can't even figure out what did her in. Her hair's been burned. But there's nothing else on her body to account f—"

"Why don't you go over her naked body inch by inch?" Goldie asked. "Take your time. Take snapshots. You men make me sick."

She left the room and returned a moment later with a blanket. She started to wrap it around Maeve. When Lachaise began to help her, she slapped his hands away. "Men." She finished the job and turned to him. "Okay. Can you put her downstairs in the cellar without trying to grab a tit?"

"What's gotten into you?"

"I just didn't like the way you started nuzzling her a few seconds after you started nuzzling me."

Paul started to laugh again. He could never quite stay a full jump ahead of Goldie's lunatic mind. He picked up the girl and carried her downstairs, arranging her on an old mattress behind some wooden cartons of canned goods. When he returned upstairs, Goldie had rolled

Regan on his back and was trying to pry up the edges of the court plaster. The adhesive had been applied imperfectly over hair and iodoform and dry blood. It came away slowly without seeming to disturb Regan too much.

"You couldn't do that to him if he were conscious," Paul said. "What's on your mind?"

"Getting out the bullet."

"Why don't we let Dr. Powers do that?"

"Because he's in Islip and Harry's here and there's Coast Guard swarming all over in between."

Paul knelt beside her and worked off another corner of the adhesive plaster. When it came away, they stared for a long time at the small, round hole. "He was shivved with a lance," Lachaise said.

Goldie's face had grown quite pale. "I'm sorry I uncovered it. Let's put some fresh stuff on. And then let's get the poor bastard across to Islip."

"Don't forget the tootsie in the cellar."

"You I can count on to do the remembering."

"I never knew you were jealous," Lachaise said. "I'm not jealous about you. What gives you the ri—"

"Why don't you just shut up and get moving?"

"All of a sudden you're willing to risk it?"

"Yeah," she agreed in a flat voice. "All of a sudden."

"Why?"

Her wide mouth tightened in a line. "Because you were right, is why. The guy is somebody special."

"What makes you say that now."

"Because." She gestured in the air, as if batting away

moths. "Because I don't know who the girl is, but he's nearly killed himself trying to get her to a doctor. And because . . ." Her voice died away. She stared gloomily at the small round wound. "Because the son-of-a-bitch was counting on me after all."

I *don't hold with the simps who shower kudos and plaudits on him. A lone wolf like Lindy scares the bejabbers out of me. That he even dreams of pulling such a stunt shows me how rare his breed is getting in this over-stuffed era of smugitude. Worse, I imagine what idiocies the great unwashed would be braying if he hadn't made it to Paree. "Darned fool lunatic! What made him think he was any better than the rest of us?" What, indeed? We hate being reminded how dirt-common most of us are.*

Harry L. Menzies
(as quoted in *Literary Digest,*
August, 1927)

Chapter 41

The land patrol commanded by Spanier had made good time moving along the bay edge of Fire Island and now had covered the few miles between the Coast Guard station and the village of Ocean Beach. Spanier was waiting at the dock when Lt. Ashley's launch arrived, bearing Maxie.

Ashley had already caught sight of Spanier when the launch was still a few hundred yards out in the bay. He felt a little odd about Spanier, who was a known friend and possible associate of Chief Heydt, which meant that he could also be in league with Harry Regan, as the Chief had evidently been.

As he supervised the tying up of the launch, Ashley wondered how closely Spanier's squad had searched for Regan. He decided that with four other men along, it would have been impossible for Spanier to deliberately miss Regan if they'd stumbled on him.

"Report," he ordered, returning Spanier's salute.

"Sir, my squad covered the distance in just under thirty minutes, along a path approximately two hundred yards wide, meeting and in some cases overlapping the patrol to our right. To date suspect has not been located."

Ashley's nostrils flared. He started to say something nasty, but decided against it. He assumed the other squads had nothing to report or he would have heard. But Regan could not possibly escape. If you sent four squads of five men each in an easterly direction along this narrow sand bar of an island, even a rabbit in its hole would be discovered.

Ashley frowned, realizing his mistake. The squads could cover the length of the island in half a day, moving fast on foot. But if Regan were under cover, really under cover, they could miss him. His own shack was demolished, as was the Purvis cottage, but there could be other homes in which he might hide.

The morning sun had grown hotter. Ashley squinted into its rays and then turned to look at Maxie, lying comfortably in the launch. Ashley wondered how welcome Harry Regan would be this morning. The night had been a complete botch. Men had died, husbands, brothers, friends. Ashley knew these people because he was one of them. Without ever putting it in so many words, he knew them to be greedy people who would put themselves out for a dollar, but not for a friend. There was something about the terrible winter along the beach, when the wind penned each of them in his own sty for weeks on end, that turned them into mean, quarrelsome people quick to take offense. It was likely that Harry Regan would be met by a blast from a shotgun if he tried to hide in any of the natives' homes.

Which left the one place he was sorry now he hadn't shaken down more thoroughly, the Fain woman's house. He'd let himself be eased out of it with a lot of kid's talk about search warrants and the like. But he was after an enemy of the public, in hot pursuit of him. And the law was clear on that point. No court orders were necessary in hot pursuit.

Ashley gestured to Spanier. "I'm staying here in Ocean Beach. Continue with your patrol."

Spanier saluted and started to about-face. "Hold it. As you were." Ashley squinted into the sun as he faced the other man. "Round up my sharpshooters. Add one of them to each patrol. That'll give us four squads of six men each. Get them assigned and then report back to me. On the double."

Ashley watched him jog off. From the launch, in a conversational tone that seemed quietly to usurp a place in what was going on, Maxie said: "You're staying in Ocean Beach, huh?"

"A little unfinished business."

"Gonna search a few houses. Smart."

"Just one."

"Goldie Fain's. Very smart."

"It's one of the few places around where he's got a chance of being taken in and hidden."

"You're not going up against that setup alone?"

"No problem."

Grunting with the effort and its effect on his wound, Maxie hoisted himself to his feet and swung up onto the dock. He stood beside Ashley and squinted into the sun in an unconscious imitation. "If you raise Regan, it'll be lots of problem."

Ashley shrugged negligently. He knew Maxie was right and he also knew he had talked himself into something of a corner by pretending to be tougher than he should be. He commanded men. He had to be prudent as well as daring. An officer was expected to know when to be each. If an officer didn't know, the men certainly couldn't be expected to figure it out for themselves.

"I think you ought to take help with you," Maxie suggested.

"I'm fine, little man. Don't worry about me."

Maxie continued to stare slit-eyed into the sun. "I know Regan. That's why I worry. He's as sneaky a devil as you'll ever meet."

"Suits me."

"Maybe we should come with you? Me and Patsy? I'm wise to Regan's tricks."

Ashley shook his head. "What good would you do me? You're my prisoners. I can't give you guns."

"Moral support."

"You're being funny."

"Two extra pairs of eyes and ears," Maxie suggested.

Ashley paused in the act of rejecting him again. Tempting. Spanier returned on the double and saluted. "Patrols enlarged, sir. They're moving off now and I've got to rejoin mine."

The mealymouthed tone he had adopted set Ashley's teeth on edge. "You'll stay right here in Ocean Beach," he ordered. "You're to accompany me on a house search."

Spanier blinked. "Yes, sir."

"Carrying handcuffs?"

"Yes, sir."

Ashley indicated the man called Patsy. "Lock him to the engine hatch."

"Yes, sir. What about the other one?"

"He comes with us."

Maxie nodded encouragingly. Ashley turned on him. "Don't think you're putting anything over on me, little man. I wouldn't trust you alone, even with the cuffs on. I haven't got anybody to guard you, so you're coming along. No other reason."

"One other, Lieutenant," Maxie assured him. "I want that bastard Regan even worse than you do."

They began walking quickly toward the Atlantic side of the island, Ashley in the lead, Spanier a step behind and Maxie struggling to keep up with them. A few of the natives hanging around Old Man Morris's general store watched them for a moment, then disappeared inside.

The morning birds had grown quiet now that the sun was well up. The sidewalks in Ocean Beach were cement, unlike the wooden boardwalks in other communities, and Ashley's leather heels made a sharp, rapping noise.

Maxie's cleated heels spattered scraping grace notes. A combination of the unusual warmth and the wound in his arm had started him sweating, something he rarely did even in summer heat.

Ashley could see the big white two-story house long before they reached it. He calculated it had at least four rooms per floor, maybe more. The two all-around decks on the first and second floors gave it the look of an old-time paddle-wheel steamer. Perhaps the designer had meant it that way to attract rich theater people. It was well known along the beach that theater people had more kale than sense. The producers and actor-drunks and shimmy dancers and what-all couldn't give away the money fast enough.

It was a shame to let dirt like that onto this island, Ashley thought. It wasn't fitting. City scum. The ocean and the sweep of the beach and dunes meant nothing to them except as a place to run around yelling and pawing each other. Let them stay in their flea-bag Broadway hotels and not contaminate this place.

He was walking faster now. He knew he had a duty to perform. There was a right way and a wrong. Thank God he still knew what was right.

He turned to Spanier. "You keep them covered."

"Them?"

"The Fain woman has one of her fancy boys there. A loudmouth named Lachaise."

"Yes, sir."

"Paul Lachaise?" Maxie asked.

Ashley turned to look at him. He'd completely forgotten the little thief was along. Come to think of it, Spanier was probably a thief, too. It didn't matter. Our Lord was crucified between two thieves and it didn't matter at all. He strode on ahead, feeling taller and more in command of himself than at any time during this whole wretched night and morning.

By God, he was going to nail Harry Regan and that was that.

He pounded up the boardwalk to the big white house and hammered on one of the doors. "Spanier, take the door on the front deck. Make sure nobody gets out that way." To Maxie he said: "Stay with me and don't try anything."

"I'm on your side, Lieutenant."

"Make damned sure you are." He pounded on the door again. "Open up!"

He could hear them inside. They seemed to be saying something to each other, not something meant for him to hear. Eventually the door opened and Lachaise stared impudently at him.

He held his hand out, palm up. "The warrant. Lay it right there."

Ashley pulled out his .45 Colt automatic and shoved it into Lachaise's abdomen. Riding him backwards, he pushed him into the house. Maxie slammed the door and all three of them were now inside.

"Like the warrant?" Ashley asked. "You've got one minute to turn Regan over to me. Or I tear this house apart."

Lachaise turned his back on Ashley and walked through the corridor to the living room. He sat down and lighted a Murad.

"Nonchalant," Goldie said. She winked at Lachaise.

"This officious baboon is giving us a minute to pull Harry Regan out of our ear," Lachaise began. "First of all, sergeant, who is that chimp you've brought with you?" He stabbed his cigarette in Maxie's direction. "Or am I just having hangover D.T.'s?"

"It's lieutenant, not sergeant," Ashley began, "and this time you're not—"

"Oh, yes, I am," Lachaise assured him. "I am still going to insist on a warrant."

"No warrant but this." Ashley showed Goldie the Colt.

"Sergeant," Lachaise smiled charmingly, "your bluff is so rotten a baby could call it."

"Try me."

"That's exactly what I intend to do," Lachaise said. "If you want to search this house, you're going to have to shoot me. And if all you do is wound me, I'm going to force you to kill me. Then you'll have to shoot the witness. Get the picture?"

Ashley shook his head. "You're too yellow for that."

"No. You are."

The two men watched each other for a moment. "Lieutenant," Maxie put in then, "I guess you know this guy has something of a rep. I mean, knocking him off is gonna get in all the papers."

Ashley turned on him. "When I ask for shit, you can come in on a stick. Not till then."

Lachaise laughed, a barking sound. "You'd better listen to him, Sergeant. He's the only one carrying a brain today."

There was a pounding at the front door. Maxie slipped sideways to let in Spanier. "Sir, everything under control?"

Ashley nodded. He hated situations like this because they forced decisions. You could always make a wrong one and then you were cooked. The whole idea of being with something like the Coast Guard, of having your own niche in something big and all-powerful, was so that you wouldn't have to make these kind of decisions and live or die by them. And now, out of the blue . . .

"Come on in, chump," Lachaise told Spanier. "In another second you're going to see me get mad and throw your little tin sergeant out on his ear."

"You won't like what a .45 does to that pretty face of yours," Ashley said somberly.

He could feel the whole thing firing up his gut again. A single central core of agony began to heat up in his colon like a flaming poker. He turned away from Lachaise and found himself looking at Maxie. He turned away from Maxie and stared at the wall.

He knew Lachaise was watching him with renewed interest. He knew they were all staring at him, even though they couldn't know what was happening inside.

"You all right, Sergeant?" Goldie piped up.

It was as if he'd swallowed a nest of rats, big slimy alley things with long scaly tails and sharp teeth and they were living inside him, gnawing at his gut from the inside. He could feel them rooting around in his vitals with their claws and teeth. He had to do something about this. Somewhere in this room was booze, he knew that. Somewhere in the house was aspirin. But he couldn't ask for either. Nor could he simply commandeer them. His position was impossible.

If he could get away for a moment. Breathe fresh air. Calm down. Get away from people like Lachaise who delighted in aggravating him. "I'll be back in a second. Just freeze." He slammed out the front door and ran down to the beach. The dune hid him for a moment from the front windows of the house. He took long, cool drafts of air. The sea breeze was salty and wet. It felt soothing.

He cursed the vermin inside him. But he knew he would triumph over them.

Chapter 42

The mattress behind the cartons of canned goods in the cellar was old and sprung and had spent too many summers on Fire Island. Harry Regan twisted painfully on his side and stared at Maeve's silent, motionless body.

He supposed he was in the worst possible shape ever. Even that one time in Pancho Villa's jail, when they were going to blindfold and shoot him at sunup, had finally turned for the better. Nothing about this could turn anything but worse.

The longer he lay doggo down here, the worse Maeve would get. She needed a doctor now, not hours from now when Ashley and his bunch got tired of waiting and left. Or else Paul's bluff wouldn't work. They'd wing Paul in the leg or something and search the house and find him. Either way Maeve would die.

He couldn't hear them upstairs any more. He had no idea how many of them there were because the walls and floors insulated him from their noise. He touched

Maeve's soft, cold face. Her cheek was as smooth as a piece of well-washed cotton.

"Maeve, darlin', you'll be fine, won't you now?"

He felt for her pulse. It was no stronger than it had been before but he decided it was a good sign that the pulse was no weaker, either.

He had to have at least one good sign. He believed in luck, of course. And he knew his had run out hours before, when the scud had parted over the moon and the hijackers and Coast Guard had closed in.

When his luck had run out, so had the luck of a lot of people who depended on him. He was pretty sure it would run out for Goldie and Paul. He was a Jonah now, and if they were smart they'd make a run for it and abandon Maeve and him.

"Maeve, you'll be all right. It's me promisin' you."

He thought she stirred. He touched her face again. It felt no warmer but he was sure she had stirred. He knew that people in physical crisis could sometimes be called back from the edge of death just by talking to them and giving them the heart to resist. He'd seen it happen. The field hospital north of Dublin, where . . .

"You're doing just grand, Maeve, just grand."

He jollied her along, letting his voice take on a bit of the brogue that she loved. She was really a darling girl, Maeve. They were all darlings, but this one loved him more. The sex was good with her, but she loved him beyond that. He wondered if he'd ever love any woman beyond the sex of it.

"You're in great shape, darlin' girl. Tiptop."

She stirred again. "Harry?"

"That's it, Maeve. It's Harry."

"I shot the black-hearted bastard." Her eyes flickered.

"That's me girl. Fire and brimstone." He patted her cheek. "Killed the miserable scut, too, ye did."

"Did I spoil it for you, Harry?"

"You're mad, woman. It's me spoilt it for you." He kissed her mouth softly. "No more talking now. Save yourself."

"Am I dying, love?"

"Not you. No chance of that," he assured her.

"Then why are you so nice to me?" Her smile was weak. "I don't care, Harry. We put in a lot of living together."

"Stop all talk."

"So if I die, at least it's been worth it." She was still for a long time.

"Maeve?"

"Sh. I'm resting."

He felt her wrist. The pulse was weak, but no weaker. Maybe he could pull them out of this yet. But he needed more than luck now. He pulled the Luger Parabellum out of its holster and yanked back the receiver slide. One 9 mm. shell lay in the chamber. The snail magazine he had lost on the ride along the beach. He had a gun with one cartridge in it.

But that was better than no gun at all.

Chapter 43

"What's eating him?" Goldie asked, staring out at the beach where Ashley stood.

"Bile." Lachaise squashed out the cigarette and turned to Maxie. "Where do you come in, young fella? On a stick, as he suggested?"

Maxie shook his head and smiled slowly. "Me you don't rile, Mr. Lachaise. I know you're real good at it." He glanced at Spanier. Then Maxie walked over to the window. He could just see Ashley on the beach. "The Lieutenant," he said, seeming to address nobody in particular, "believes that Chief Heydt and Harry Regan were in cahoots. He's convinced of it, for now."

No one responded. Goldie yawned. Maxie turned around. "I'm not boring you or nothing, am I?"

"Me? I'm just sleepy," Goldie said.

"But it's only a matter of time," Maxie went on in his peculiarly undirected way, "before he tumbles to the

whole layout. Even somebody as stupid as him. So, before that happens, I think we need us a massacre."

Lachaise stood up. "What the hell are you babbling
about?"

"Don't that make sense?" Maxie asked the air. "They
all go and we hang it on Regan. We hang everything
on Regan. Okay?"

"Who are you talking to?" Goldie asked.

"Okay," Spanier said.

He lowered his Springfield from port-arms position
and pointed it at Lachaise. "Sit back down on the sofa,
prettyboy. You, lady, sit next to him."

"Right," Maxie agreed. "And when Ashley comes back
he sits next to her."

Goldie sat beside Paul. "I don't get it, honey. Do you?"
Her words were a bit slurred from the two heavy drinks
she had had half an hour before.

"These two are buddies. They're going to shoot us
and Ashley."

"Are you absolutely positive?"

"Absitively, Mr. Gallagher," Lachaise said.

"Posilutely, Mr. Shean." Goldie giggled and pointed at
Maxie. "He's sure a short portion of poison, huh?"

"As long as he rids the world of Ashley, he's aces in
my book."

Maxie laughed abruptly. "Mr. Lachaise, you got class."

"How come you're not worried about the publicity of
killing us?" Paul wanted to know. "It stopped Ashley."

"He's in a different end of the business," Maxie explained, not unkindly. "In my end, publicity don't hurt. It even helps when people know that, let's say, if they don't do what we want, they get killed."

"His end and your end. Business associates?"

"In a way." Maxie laughed again. His small, jockey's frame seemed to spruce up and brighten, adding an inch in height thereby. "I mean, without my end of it, he'd be out of a job."

Lachaise pointed a finger. "But it's more than that, isn't it? I mean, you actually have him in your pocket. You pay him off. That sort of thing."

"Not this chump. Just some of his boys." Maxie nodded at Spanier.

"But, maybe I'm still not saying it right," Lachaise persisted in a friendly, argumentative way, as if they were discussing the merits of several major league outfielders. "In other words, between your bunch and his bunch, you rule the world. There's getting to be less and less space in between you for people to breathe."

"Very nice," Maxie said. "You think straight, Mr. Lachaise."

He took the Springfield from Spanier and laid it across his knees.

"And there's really no such thing as opposites," Paul went on, more to himself than to anyone in the room. "It's all a matter of orbits. Any of us in orbit with you and with him are going to get squeezed to death. Opposites meet. On a circle, everything meets. You need

294

each other, you and he, and you reach out and you meet. Very interesting."

Maxie nodded appreciatively. "It's real sad you have to go, Mr. Lachaise."

Goldie sat up straighter. "What is all this, anyway? He isn't really gonna kill us?"

"He's got to," Paul assured her. "He can't trust us not to squeal on him."

"That's not true," Maxie said. "We got other ways of keeping people quiet. We got hooks into people like you that you probably don't even know about." He was getting carried away now by his own words. "I mean, we put money in shows. We own theaters. If we said you don't work on Broadway, lemme tell you, you wouldn't work."

Lachaise wrinkled his nose. "Ah, that's all sissy stuff. The only good witness is a dead witness."

"I gotta admit you're right, Mr. Lachaise. Sorry."

They heard Ashley's footsteps coming up the stairs from the beach. "Okay," Maxie said. "No funny stuff. You get it nice and neat either way, but I hate funny stuff."

"Ashley's got a gun," Goldie pointed out.

"You or Mr. Lachaise say one word and he gets it as he comes in the door. Before he has a chance to pull that .45."

They could hear Ashley's footsteps on the deck now. He threw open the front door and walked in. He frowned and stopped in his tracks.

"What's going on?"

Maxie pointed the Springfield at his heart. "Spanier," he said, "get around behind the Lieutenant and take away that Colt of his, okay?" As Spanier started to move, Maxie added: "Don't get between him and me, or you both eat lead."

In absolute silence, Spanier lifted the unstrapped holster flap and eased out the Colt. He hefted the heavy automatic for a moment, then stepped backwards away from Ashley.

"Very good," Maxie said. "Lieutenant, go sit down by Miss Fain."

"What is the meaning of this?"

Maxie began to laugh. "Very good. Lovely." He jerked the muzzle of the Springfield toward the sofa and Ashley sat down beside Goldie.

"Now we got only one problem left," Maxie said. "If they're found with Springfield slugs in them, would that be the type of ammo Harry Regan would use? Or should we take them out with the Colt? Regan's Luger has a slug only a little smaller than the .45. So, Spanier, see how neat you can do it."

"You mean me?" Spanier looked down at the Colt.

"You. Now."

Spanier moistened his lips. "Maxie," he began, "when me and Heydt made our deal, there wasn't anything in it about this. Just information, you said. That's all you wanted. Advance information. Nothing about killing anybody."

"There is now. The deal's changed."

"I don't know. It's not right."

The Springfield jerked in Maxie's arms. The slug tore through Spanier's cheek and coursed upward through his brain before it blew out his left temple in a spout of red.

The rifle swung sideways to cover the people on the sofa. "Hipshot," Maxie said. "Didn't even aim."

"You're quite a headshooter, huh?" Lachaise asked. His lips looked white around the edges. "That's not as easy as it looks."

"You're absolutely right, Mr. Lachaise." Maxie sidled over to Spanier and took the Colt out of his hand. "I'm a regular two-gun rootin' tootin' headshooter." The slanting sun set his smile on fire.

"Look here," Ashley said. He seemed to have some difficulty getting out the words. "I thought we had a deal."

"We? Us, Lieutenant?"

"What good does it do you to kill me? I'm the only one who can do anything about Regan for you. Nobody'd believe you. They'd believe me."

"Regan is my personal meat, Lieutenant. Just because I strung you along a little doesn't mean we had any deal. What do I need you for? I got only one thing left to do: put Regan's head in a box and take it to Brooklyn."

The roar of the heavy cartridge made Goldie wince. Maxie's head snapped back and blood gushed from his mouth. Lachaise leaped up and turned around to stare into the darkened hallway. It was impossible to see anything in there because the sun was in his eyes.

"Harry?"

Regan moved slowly into the room, the Parabellum pointed at Ashley. "Pick up the whole bloody arsenal, Paul, me lad." He sat down opposite Ashley. "Is it you, Ashley?"

Ashley stared at him. "You're Regan." It was not a question.

Regan closed his eyes for a moment and waited for the pain in his chest to subside. "I had to hold the gun in both hands and it's got a nasty recoil that way."

"I've got a boat hidden," Lachaise said.

"Be kind enough to pick up the estimable Miss Curran in the cellar like a good man." Regan accepted the Colt and let the Springfield lie on his lap. "Carry her to the boat and Goldie will carry me right after. First tie up this hopeless idiot."

"You won't get away with this," Ashley said.

"I'd have a hell of a better chance if I left you dead, wouldn't I?"

Ashley nodded. "They'll find me here eventually. And I'll tell them where you are."

Regan shook his head. "Paul, please get a move on." He turned to Ashley. "You don't know where we're going."

"A doctor, from the look of you."

Regan grimaced. "You're making it awful hard not to kill you, Ashley. What makes you so perverse?"

Ashley's face was red. "There's a right and there's a wrong. I do what's right, even if it means I die."

Regan shook his head slowly. "You poor, demented lunatic." He gestured to Goldie. "Tie his hands behind him, sweetheart." He watched her for a moment. "You made a deal with this scum here." He prodded Maxie with the toe of his boot. "Is that doing what's right?"

"The results are what count. I made a deal with him to get you."

"And that justified making the deal." Regan nodded. "I know your kind of mind, Ashley. It starts out judging everything, because you always know what's right and what's wrong."

"I'm happy to admit that. Happy."

"And of course, the next step is that you only do what's right. But the last step is that whatever you do is right. I know that kind of logic. It leads to all the terrible things men do to each other because they only do what's right."

"Don't justify your own crimes, Regan."

Harry watched as Goldie finished tying the Lieutenant. "I've run into your kind." His eyes lit up. "Tell me Lieutenant, do you suffer from constipation? Ever have any stomach problems?" Harry's eyes raked sideways across Ashley's face. "Am I right? Do you? Confess."

"Why not just shoot me?"

Goldie stood up from the sofa. "It's almost as if he's asking for it."

Regan stood up slowly, saving himself. "Of course he's asking for it. He wants it. Death is his way out."

"Harry, that's crazy."

Regan nodded. "Let's let the poor bastard alone." He handed her the Springfield. "Lead the way."

"Regan!" Ashley called.

"Try to take it easy, Lieutenant." They moved out the front door, Goldie still in her white lounging pajamas with the long Isadora Duncan scarf and the Navy-issue Springfield, Regan in his bloody shirt and jeans with the Luger in its holster and the Colt hanging from his left hand.

"Regan!"

"Hear that?" Regan asked Goldie. "He's saying 'kill me!' That's what he means. And he means it with all his heart."

Goldie led the way down the stairs to the beach. It was well after eight in the morning and there had been several gunshots, but the wind had probably carried them away without anyone's hearing them.

"*Regan!*"

Goldie and Regan moved west along the base of the dune and entered the no-man's-land beyond Ocean Beach. They hurried along the deserted path to the bay where Paul had already put Maeve, in her blanket, in the bottom of the runabout. He was fitting the knotted length of clothesline into the Evinrude's starter flywheel. He glanced up to see them coming. He pulled out the choke button. Bracing himself, he gave the line a smooth, quick pull. The motor caught and roared into life.

The runabout was starting to move as Goldie helped Regan into it. They all crouched low as Paul swung the tiller handle on the outboard and sent the boat crashing through a series of whitecaps, its bow aimed at Islip water tower across the bay.

The morning breeze whipped spray in Harry Regan's face. His chest wound ached as he breathed the air. He bent over Maeve and felt her throat. The pulse was steady. He looked up in time to see Goldie watching him with a dark, forlorn look. He grinned at her. After a long moment, she grinned back, a little.

Chapter 44

It took Ashley about half an hour to work out of the knots
Goldie had tied. He stood up from the white wicker sofa
and rubbed his wrists. Then he glanced at his watch.
With the exception of one or two men left at the Coast
Guard station, his entire force was deployed in squads
moving eastward along the length of Fire Island on a
damned fool wild goose chase.

He walked to the front windows and stared at the
ocean. There was a small craft out there, probably one
of the private fishing boats that occasionally seined where
the big trawlers did.

Ashley looked around him. He had to do something.
Get to the telephone in town. Alert the station. Do something.

Instead he switched on the radio. It was one of the old
Aeriola Juniors, a small, square black box with a hinged
top. He opened the set and looked down at the lever that
controlled the tuning condenser. He clamped the ear-

phones on his head and swung the lever slowly through its wide arc.

". . . what'll I do, when you are far from me and—"

". . . glorious achievement of mankind may be coming to a triumphant conclusion. We'll know more in a few hours, but at this moment, Charles Augustus Lindbergh is seven hours past the halfway point in his epoch-making flight. We have a report in from a Norwegian freighter in the North Atlantic that sighted him at dawn this morning some five hundred miles south of Iceland. He seemed to be having no trouble at all and even waggled the wings of the *Spirit of St. Louis* as he passed overhead. However, it's still a long way to—"

Ashley pulled the earphones off his head. He switched off the radio and sank down on the sofa beside it. He realized he was very tired.

He supposed Lindbergh would make it. He supposed the world needed Lindberghs. The man wasn't any higher rank than he, actually.

There was some point, he guessed, to the fact that the race depended on freakish people like Lindbergh. But what might be all right for one eccentric wasn't right for everybody.

Ashley intended to do the right thing. "Even if it kills me," he said aloud.

He shocked himself by speaking aloud. This was no way to act. The pain in his stomach had abated slightly to the point where it was almost bearable. He got up and rummaged around the living room until he found the almost empty bottle of Johnny Walker Black Label. He opened it and upended it into his mouth. After a long, hard pull, he capped the bottle and sat down on the sofa again.

It was funny that Regan hadn't killed him. Regan was absolutely not what he had expected. He'd had him all wrong. When it came right down to it, Regan had saved his life.

He got up and went to the window. He sat in the chair there and studied the heavy brass and copperbound telescope. The optics were old-fashioned and not as powerful as his own smaller binoculars.

He lifted the telescope and aimed it at the tiny craft now moving farther out to sea. She sprang into instant focus. A beamy boat, waddling like a duck. Nobody aboard. There was even a rag of a sail on her stubby mast and she was very busily making her way toward Portugal. He could read the name on her stern. *"Dearie."* Something like it.

She was heavy laden, but she seemed to spring forward to meet each wave. It would break over her long-sprited bow and the bright sunlight would shower down jewels. She looked free and easy and headed for adventure and life and all the warm, good things he would never have. It was going to be a beautiful day.

Ashley let the telescope drop to his knees. He felt as if he had lost something very, very important. He doubled over the telescope, cuddling it against him, and began to weep bitterly.

The eagle's lonely flight from west to east, impertinent mockery of the Sun God's daily journey, has opened a profound abyss between what was and what will be. Never again will man be as he was. A seal has been set upon an era. The new one that opens before us bears the chilling breath of chaos and doom.

Ravi Chandralal Rau
(as quoted in the N.Y. *World*,
May 22, 1927)

ABOUT THE AUTHOR

LESLIE WALLER wrote his first published novel at the age of nineteen, and since then he has worked as a newspaperman and a public-relations executive while completing several outstanding novels, including *The Banker* (a Literary Guild selection), *Phoenix Island,* and *The Family.* A University of Chicago graduate with an M.A. from Columbia University, Mr. Waller now lives and works in New York City with his wife and two teen-age daughters, spending their summers in New Milford, New York. He has recently resigned his public-relations position to devote full time to writing.